THE SKATER

By Rob Rodger

Copyright © 2012 by Rob Rodger
First Edition – November 2012

This book is a work of fiction. Names, characters, businesses, organizations, places, events and incidents either are the product of the author's imagination or are used fictitiously. Any resemblance to actual persons, living or dead, events, or locales is entirely coincidental.

ISBN
978-1-4602-0453-5 (Hardcover)
978-1-4602-0451-1 (Paperback)
978-1-4602-0452-8 (Ebook)

All rights reserved.

No part of this publication may be reproduced in any form, or by any means, electronic or mechanical, including photocopying, recording, or any information browsing, storage, or retrieval system, without permission in writing from the publisher.

Published by:

FriesenPress
Suite 300 – 852 Fort Street
Victoria, BC, Canada V8W 1H8

www.friesenpress.com

Distributed to the trade by The Ingram Book Company

This book is dedicated to my son, Kenny, who inspired me to continue with it even though he never got the opportunity to read it. He was an inspiration to all who knew him and all who knew him loved him and he left no one untouched by his GIANT spirit.

CHAPTER 1

The details are a little sketchy but it appears Johnny Collier's northern Ontario upbringing wasn't the very best. Nevertheless, he wasn't tortured or brutalized. He was, though, reared with an iron fist wielded by his unwieldy and wild drunken father. Times were tough but made even tougher by Mr. Peter Collier's wanton disregard for most anything except his booze. When Johnny got in the way, Johnny paid the price. When his sister, Sylvia, got in the way, Johnny still paid the price.

It seemed the only thing Johnny was good at was hockey. No wonder, lakes were frozen nearly six months a year and all the boys played hockey. If they could afford a pair of skates, that is. Johnny's mother, Hazel, saw to it that every year Johnny got a used pair of skates. At least they were the right size, even if they were a little worn. It made little difference because Johnny was always, literally and figuratively, head and shoulders above the other players. He always seemed to find himself on travelling teams, which he was ecstatic about but which really irked his father. Money was always the issue when he played on travelling teams. His father didn't like that for one reason. It cut into his drinking money. He pretty much had to give up a whole case of stock ale every week in the winter just so 'the punk' could have fun wasting his time playing hockey. "He ain't goin' nowhere anyway!" Peter screamed at his wife on more than one occasion. Still, she lobbied for her son and she, too, paid the price. Usually, she paid on Saturday nights when the Leafs lost. Luckily for her, in those days they didn't lose too often.

As the years passed, Johnny's skill level just kept rising. His father died of cirrhosis of the liver when he was seventeen. He didn't cry at his father's funeral. He didn't attend it. He and his mother decided he shouldn't break stride for someone who didn't care much about him anyway. So, off he went to play hockey and curse his father with every shift on the ice. A scout for the Detroit Red Wings was impressed enough with his play to recommend him to the team management for a try-out. He would be eighteen by the time training camp started. Johnny anticipated his try-out just about every waking moment. He was bigger than the average NHL'er even then. He was tall, strong and fast with great stick handling ability, a great shot and consummate skating skills. He had it all. Or, so he thought.

When the day came for his shot at the big time his coach drove him to the train station in North Bay, where he departed for Toronto. He hung around the Queen Street station for a couple of hours until it was time to go and get on the bus for Windsor. He had never been this far from home before, alone, and he was feeling a little insecure. He thought about his girlfriend, Edith, and that gave him some comfort. On his second last night before leaving he and Edith had finally 'done it'. The fact that they had to do it out in the woods didn't bother Johnny at all. Edith would have preferred a warm bed but she went ahead with it anyway because she was insecure herself. After all, her boyfriend was going to be in a big American city. And he would be alone. Would he meet someone else? What if he did? Would she lose him to the NHL?

"That Collier kid's got a shit load o' talent!" Murray, the scout said.

"And a hell of an attitude," said Coach Lemmon.

Johnny impressed all and sundry with his skills but his very short fuse and hot headedness didn't endear him to the coach at all. Lemmon already had enough muscle on his team. He didn't need any more, no matter how good this kid was. He knew his talent was sufficient but, Lemmon thought, he just needed a bit more maturity. He told Johnny all this, and he told him to come back next year and give it another go. He said the Wings would be in touch. Johnny was stunned. He couldn't believe it. He knew he was good enough, tough enough and fast enough. All those many hours to get back home he ruminated, talking to himself on the train like some kind of Tourette's tourist. "Mature a little bit? So, I broke his nose? Fuckin' pansy anyway."

Despite Johnny's anger and disappointment, his mother and girlfriend seemed to take it in stride and held out hope for the next season. Johnny was pissed off, really pissed off. So much so that his hockey career was starting to go off the rails. He finally just quit after his second suspension for clubbing an opponent with a two hander right across his mouth. Blood and teeth and splinters were everywhere. A huge brawl ensued and Johnny's organized playing days were over. He consoled himself with the thought that at least he didn't have to listen to his father. He almost organically hated the old man. And with the old man gone, at least he could move on with his life. Besides, he could still get together with his buddies and play a pick up game any time he wanted. He planned to get a job driving a truck. He thought about, maybe, marrying Edith and settling down one day.

That day was to materialize very soon. Edith was pregnant. "Holy shit!" How did he go from potential hockey stardom to just a working stiff with a wife and a kid on the way so fast? Well, at least he could take off and get half snapped to celebrate, just like dear old dad. Unfortunately, Johnny wasn't in any way, shape or form aware of the psychological forces at work in his psyche and on his personality. He would, twenty odd years later, die ignorant of some very basic realities. He didn't see that what he loved he tended to worship. What he loved he cared for, looked after, protected and even over protected. However, what he hated, truly hated, was his father and he, like all the others, would always become what he hated. Johnny had become his father, broken, frustrated and angry. And, just like dear old dad, he too would soon have his very own whipping boy.

Johnny moved Edith and Henry to southern Ontario when Henry was two years old. Edith enjoyed the weather, especially the winters, which were considerably shorter and warmer than the winters she had grown up enduring. Being a truck driver, Johnny had made a few long hauls to the St. Catharines area and heard about job opportunities at the GM plant. He was finally hired about a year and a half later. The biggest disappointment for Edith was not ever having enough money for a down payment on a house. It should have been a slam dunk, considering the wages were good at GM and houses were cheap in St. Catharines. But when the only breadwinner in the house was also the insatiable beer drinker in the house, the house would always be a rental.

Henry was small and slight from the start and while Edith referred to him as wiry, Johnny saw his son as just plain scrawny. By the time Henry was fifteen he knew full well what his father thought of him. Try as he did to curry favor with the old man, he was never able to overcome his deep feelings of insecurity and worthlessness. By this time, Henry had a young sister six years his junior. Nancy, it seemed to Henry, could do no wrong in Johnny's eyes. If Henry had only understood that his father was caught between compulsively reliving his own childhood and assuming the persona of his abusive father. He would protect Nancy as he had done with Sylvia, and he would abuse Henry as his father had done with him. So, it wasn't Henry's fault that, in spite of his diminutive size, he became a practised and skilled bully and abuser in his own right. Out of his own self-loathing grew a malicious ability to manipulate. Nothing pleased him more than tormenting bigger boys. It was classic. He hated his father for never appreciating him. So, when the opportunity arose to, in some way, hurt a young surrogate he always enjoyed the feeling of power it gave him.

As with so many families of their ilk the Colliers lived through comparison, which inevitably bred envy and resentment in them all. These pervasive feelings touched everyone in the household, but none more so than young Henry. The anger within him, born of fear and insecurity, was covertly encouraged by both his parents as their marital devolution found its own path to expression. Johnny felt trapped and Edith was trapped. Actually, Henry's father enjoyed hearing of his exploits with his friends because only at those moments could he live vicariously through his emaciated looking son. For fleeting seconds Johnny felt something close to pride at the idea that his boy could control others. While Edith became more embittered, Johnny grew more frustrated and violent. Henry was emboldened.

Edith, whose intelligence far exceeded her husband's, sought a perverse comfort in her deviousness. Johnny never really knew what hit him when it came to his wife. She had developed a Svengali like way of pacifying her partner. She always managed to keep the ball moving, so to speak, so that Johnny was always unaware of her real motives. Her most effective technique was using other people as scapegoats for his frustration and anger. Unbeknownst to Johnny he, in fact, was hers. She could have done much better than marry this loser, she thought. Only her fear kept her from leaving. Her cowardice fueled her bitterness and she could not see that she was the only one to blame for her misery.

Given Johnny's background he really didn't have a hope of coping with Edith's underhanded onslaughts. She could deftly turn his annoyance with her toward someone else in a mere moment. Undermining him financially became a game for her and the more bamboozled he was, the more perversely pleased she was. Once in awhile, usually on weekends when Johnny was well into his third case of beer, his rage would spill over and Edith would somehow manage to redirect his anger from herself to Henry. Soon after Henry had become the focus of his father's violence, Edith would play the martyr by intervening on Henry's behalf. Henry's gratitude for his mother's interventions would have soured quickly had he known the truth.

So, it wasn't any wonder that Henry's dark side began to expand exponentially in this cauldron of unhappiness that the neighbors knew only as 234 Racine St. One of Henry's favorite ploys was to ingratiate himself into a group by using his quick wit, for he was quick witted and very intelligent. He would at some point disingenuously, after having manufactured a crisis, stand up to someone not belonging to his group. This served two purposes. First, his friends were endeared to him, thinking he was courageous. Second, it usually resulted in a fight. And someone would invariably be injured. Every single time this occurred one of Henry's bigger friends would stand up for him. This was the protection he craved from his father. Satisfied that he had engineered everything and manipulated everyone, he could then boast about how he helped fight the bad guys.

Just like his father was and his mother had become, Henry was totally ruled by his ego. Of course he didn't know it because that was the secret power of his ego, to make him perceive and believe it to be himself. In fact, nothing could have been further from the truth. Henry had very little awareness, if any at all. Any tiny glimpse of reality was far too frightening to accept, never mind endure. He might have set himself free if the spark had been somewhat larger but the flint of his soul was drenched with the blood of his boyhood. His fate was sealed. For Henry, life was surely a game of tag. "You're it, pass it on," he mouthed those words frequently. The curse of generations since Adam had befallen Henry Collier. He was doomed to live an empty life and die a hollow death. He was the ultimate user. But unlike his his father and grandfather his drug of choice was people. Sure, he drank and drugged and smoked but his addiction was the oldest of all. He was addicted to power itself and the more mean-spirited he became, the greater the fix needed to satisfy him.

As his humanity shrank, so too did the humans around him shrink away and leave. They could not bear to be ravaged any longer. He fed on their weaknesses for his own malicious gratification. His skill lay in constantly keeping his friends off guard. Not only did he play one against the other but each against themselves. This misguided talent he learned from his mother; cajole, be kind, inspire, then plant doubt. Ungrounded people had no defense against this kind of psychic warfare. Their egos too ruled their lives. In reacting with a strong emotion the ego always won. Through recognition, awareness and consciousness the animal side of himself could have been tamed but without any objective examination Henry was doomed to suffer a life reacting to implanted commands.

The excitement of his manipulations was the certain knowledge that no one knew he had orchestrated all the frustrations, fights and emotional chaos. As long as his complicity remained secret he could never be judged and that was one of his greatest fears. Always making fools of the weaker lads, he would nevertheless still find ways to humiliate the stronger ones. He was an outright hypnotist, a master magician. At fifteen he was the consummate con artist. What would become of this selfish and pernicious young instigator?

Decent women with a spot of common sense could see right through Henry. So, his proclivity for female companionship saw its expression with a certain singular type. That type was more than exemplified by his current concubine, Charlene Kempf-Klassen. She met Henry in San Fransisco at a psychiatric convention. Charlene was the product of a wealthy family of diamond merchants originally from Cape Town. The patriarch of her family, Gerry Kempf, had cashed out of the mining business years ago and added to the family's fortune by diversifying. He became involved with an international hotel chain, the alternate energy industry and served on the boards of numerous corporations. Had Charlene not been guileless, she would have never entertained the idea of a serious relationship with Henry.

Henry emigrated to the United States to abandon all connections with his life as he had known it. His father died an alcoholic's death before Henry turned twenty two. His mother acquiesced to pay for the rest of his education with most of the life insurance money. Edith seemed to flourish in the absence of the alcoholic tyranny she had suffered for so long yet Henry still found her pull on him to be unsettling. Was a move out of the country and as far away as possible Henry's way of breaking free? It seemed so.

As a psychologist Henry well understood his own personality problems but as a child of the dusk he could not bear honest self-examination. To do so would have meant shining the light of truth on the foundational lie that was his entire life. His self-awareness was at a lower ebb now than it had ever been, partly due to his psychological schooling. He used any trick at his disposal to distance himself from the knowledge of his power source. Pretending to be something he wasn't was second nature to him. As the years passed he could not differentiate between his ego and his conscience because the latter had long since been buried.

Charlene, on the other hand, was long on brains but short on common sense. Common sense wasn't so common after all. An intelligent woman who had used her native ability to excel in her field she was, though, open, honest and naïve. Her naïveté was the reason she believed her man, Henry, was a good and caring man. She understood, only too well, that many of her patients had twisted psyches moulded by various trauma but she wasn't cynical enough to consider the possibility that one of her own elite group might be likewise troubled. That she didn't notice Henry drank too much was not entirely her fault. Concealment was a trademark of not only the alcoholic but the psychopathic personality as well. His secretive personality manifested in ways far beyond his drinking.

They had been romantically involved for almost a year before Charlene discovered that Henry's mother was alive and well and living in Niagara Falls. Up to that point she had been led to believe that the woman was dead. When she confronted him Henry deftly explained that his mother was a drunk and a junkie and that she lived on government assistance, supplemented by turning tricks in the honeymoon capital. Of course, every word of it was bunk but Charlene had no reason not to believe him, being convinced by Henry's disingenuous histrionics and false tears.

The Skater

Because Henry's practice was in Baton Rouge he was able to keep Charlene at a distance, so to speak. The hospital in Shreveport, where she worked, necessitated that she live in reasonably close proximity to it. The possibility of both of them commuting from somewhere equidistant to the two cities was discussed and discarded. Henry vowed to himself, years earlier, never to live with anyone again. This relationship with Charlene was proving to have a lot of potential but their work locations would preclude living together continuously. That, Henry could handle. So far, he had managed to keep Charlene from even visiting his home, always deferring to her and making the drive up to Shreveport. But he knew this couldn't last. Cohabiting on the weekends would be a sacrifice he would grudgingly make. The fact that Charlene's family was wealthy and influential had not escaped him. He enjoyed living luxuriously and a little extra privilege was welcomed.

Owing to his particular and ominous personality traits, Henry could not and would not view his career as an end in and of itself. Most people viewed his station and its trappings as evidence of his having arrived, but his desire to infiltrate, instigate and manipulate drove him to unconscionable lengths, both in his practice and in his personal ambition. He loved tinkering with people's minds and on more than one occasion he used what he described as passive hypnosis. In other words, the patient had no knowledge of being hypnotized. After all, this had always been Henry's classic modus operandi.

CHAPTER 2

One warm Tuesday afternoon after seeing his youngest patient, a ten year old with ADD, Henry received a very interesting and promising phone call.

"Hello", Henry said.

"Hello, Mr. Collier, how are you?" asked Calvin Heinbecker.

"Fine thanks," Henry responded.

"Mr. Collier, my name is Cal Heinbecker. I'm with the Jacksonville Jaguars. I'm the team physician, and I wonder if I could ask you a few questions?"

"Sure, go right ahead. I'm a big football fan, but I gotta warn you. I'm a Saints fan all the way," Henry boasted.

"Well, I guess in a way everyone's a Saints fan, Mr. Collier."

"Please, call me Henry."

"Okay. Henry, I guess if you follow football you know we've been struggling a bit lately."

"Yeah, well, hopefully things'll turn around for you."

"Well, Henry, that's kind of why I'm calling. You see, our owner thinks it might be a good idea to consider hiring a performance consultant, and we've compiled a list of people and you're on that list. So, we were wondering if you'd consider coming in for an interview."

"Me? I'm, uh, speechless."

"Don't be speechless Henry, talk to me."

"Are you serious?"

"Very serious Henry or I wouldn't be calling you," Cal said.

"Well, I've got a pretty busy practice goin' here. How much time would be involved in this..... consulting?"

"How much time? You don't even have the job yet. I think you're jumpin' the gun here, Henry."

"Never hurts to ask," Henry replied.

"Alright, it would probably be one day a week, every other week, pretty much, during the regular season."

"One day every other week? I've got to think about it. I can't say for sure right now. I'd have to get back to you. Is that okay? And listen, is this private consultation or group work?"

"Private, so I'm told. One-on-one with some selected players. How does that sound?"

The wheels were already spinning in Henry's head as he envisioned what this opportunity could do for him. "Sounds good."

"If you can let us know by Friday we can start scheduling interviews next week," Cal told him.

"I can certainly do that. One question though."

"Shoot."

"There's a hell of a lot of psychologists in this country, sports or otherwise. Why would you call me? I've only been down here a couple of years. I'm surprised I'd even be on your radar."

"Well, you're on somebody's," Cal said.

"Hmm," Henry sighed.

"Anyway, Henry. It's been good talkin' to you. Let me give you my number, and you can let me know whichever way you go."

The sound of the phone clicking into its cradle never sounded so sweet. He stared at it for a few seconds in silence. What an opportunity, he thought. He always loved football. In fact, he was passionate about most sports. Football was a game that, unfortunately, he'd always been too small to play. This would be an opportunity to not only live vicariously through the players but to have some measure of control over them as well. This was the first time he wished, since his father died, that he was still alive. Caught up in his dream, he allowed himself the latitude to chide the old man and gloat a little too. The old alkie couldn't cut the mustard in the big-time, but the mustard seed would grow wildly in the rich and fertile fields of the NFL. His imagination ran rampant with visions of rich athletes, parties, women, booze and drugs. Why wouldn't these guys want to invite him into their circle? After all, he was going to get to know them quite intimately and, more important, they would be beholden to him. But he didn't have the job yet, so he decided right then and there to saturate himself with the NFL network for the next little while. Maybe he could even find out who his competition was.

"Hello?"

"Hey Char. Busy?"

"I've got a couple of minutes," Charlene answered.

"You'll never guess where I'm goin' next week."

"Where?"

"Jacksonville."

"Why?" Charlene feigned.

"Got an interview with the Jaguars."

"They need an offensive shrink?"

"No, they need a team shrink."

"Yeah, I know," Charlene told him.

"How do you know?" Henry was surprised and deflated.

"Yeah, talked to them a while ago. Told them no thanks. Figured you'd be interested though," Charlene said.

"Did you give them my number?"

"No, never thought."

"Well, anyway I think I've got a good shot," he said.

"Pretty confident," she said.

"No reason not to be."

"Well, Henry that's great, but I've gotta go now. Okay? I'll call you later. Love you."

"Okay, bye."

Henry recorded every single minute of the NFL network from that point forward until Friday. He even cancelled lunch dates to go home and watch TV. If there was one thing Henry excelled at it was focusing 100% on something until it was second nature or solved or, at least, he was as fully prepared as he could be. He acquainted himself with some of the football jargon, training techniques and statistics. He generally became more conversant with football in its entirety. He learned of trades, both past and impending. He knew who had shown what at the combine. He began to understand more about how teams do their business. So much preparation and effort and energy and, of course, time went into preparing and executing a full season. In his chameleon like fashion he was beginning to transform himself. At the very least when he appeared for his interview they would know he had prepared himself. As far as his experience, talent and professionalism were concerned, he would blow them away.

This is how his 'game plan' would be executed. A paper resume, pristinely typed, would be submitted. It would be a typical resume for someone in his profession with mostly arid yet accurate facts and figures designed to cure insomnia. Added to the obvious list of credentials, postings and experience he would include a single sheet of paper. It would be handwritten, as if it had been an afterthought. On this handwritten page the names of two disparate and very different individuals would be listed. The two named individuals would have nothing whatsoever to do with contact sports or team sports. One name would be that of a male and the other a female. A figure skater and a downhill skier would win the day for Henry, the part-time imposter.

He never ever knew where his life would lead him but he always knew that if he took care to visualize, prepare and then act he would be successful. Like the thief in the night, the tumblers would all click into place, opening the safe and delivering unto Henry his rightful bounty. Since his college days he had meticulously cataloged people of interest to him. His reasoning was sound, as far as he was concerned. One day, he might be able to profit from his foresight, and it was beginning to look like he would. The prophet motive was what he called this obsession of his. The one useful thing his father taught him was that a great player always out-anticipates the competition. His father told him that it didn't matter what the sport was. The rule was always the same. Henry extrapolated this basic tenet into every aspect of his life. His father was only a has been hockey player who never really was and so he was unable to apply his philosophy in any other area. Henry thought like a judo champion, always using the opponent's force to put him in the position he wanted. In a perverse way, he was sure his father would have been proud of him.

Years earlier, in college, he had an epiphany during a conversation with a friend. His friend was always talking about getting rich by doing this or that or investing in something or other. His friend mentioned that big companies needed to protect their domain names. That's when Henry had his dusky brainstorm. He procured for himself a half dozen generically titled websites. His idea was that these sites could provide him background cover for whatever purpose was necessary. There was no more shape or form to this idea than devious future intentions alone. He was just positioning himself for any unlikely potentialities. He was out-anticipating the opponent, whomever that might prove to be.

So now it was time for Henry to backtrack into his websites, after double and triple checking all the facts about the two sports stars in question. This was where his foresight proved invaluable to him. In creating these websites many years earlier, he circumvented anyone who would have reason to verify the birth dates of the sites by making them appear historical, and therefore legitimate. He was also able to insert himself into phony newspaper articles listed on the sites. The articles had links to newspaper sites, just in case someone decided to verify that the articles did, indeed, originate from that source. Some of the links weren't real but were sites that he'd also created years earlier. He had also been careful, during their creation, to stagger their startup dates. And so he set about to alter the historical record, so the record played was the song of his choosing.

Deborah Dececchi was a wealthy woman owing to her father's very hard work, very long foresight and very good luck. In 1910 Mario Dececchi emigrated to the United States with his two older sisters and his parents. His father, Dino Dececchi came to America with his family to pursue a better life for everyone. Dino was a shoemaker of considerable skill, but he worked very hard for very little. He wasn't the only shoemaker in New York, but life was still better than back in Naples. Here, he thought, Mario and his sisters would thrive. They would speak good English, like an American, and be rich like one too.

Mario helped out with his father's business throughout his school years, and by the time he left school to work in a restaurant he knew most everything about shoemaking and shoe repair. The restaurant paid him twice the amount of money his father could afford to pay him. But he still worked extra hours in the shoe shop, for his father.

Working in the restaurant was an apprenticeship that would eventually be the foundation of Mario's success. He began washing dishes before learning the art and science of waiting tables. He also helped in the kitchen when required and gleaned much from his mentors in the process. By the time Mario was twenty-six he had become the maitre d' at The Palace, one of the finest restaurants in New York. A mere three years later, he was named the assistant to the assistant manager. Life was getting better and better in so many ways for Mario after losing both his sisters and his mother in a tragic car accident the year before. When his father died in his sleep six months after the accident, Mario would have been inconsolable were it not for Amanda Palmer, his girlfriend and new owner of The Palace. She had inherited the restaurant from her father after the stock market crashed in 1929. Charles Palmer had lost his entire fortune, save for his restaurant, and he couldn't bear the thought of the humiliation he would suffer. So, like so many others at the time who were financially ruined, he took his own life, leaving the restaurant to Amanda.

Of course, with the sudden death of his own father, Mario also became a business owner. Vexed as he was over the future of his father's shop he, nonetheless, listened to Amanda's advice and retained the business. Working full-time in the restaurant, and almost full-time as a shoemaker, Mario's ambition and drive to succeed only increased. From the tragedy of the automobile accident grew a realization that traffic accidents and fatalities were on the increase all over the United States. He knew why. Because traffic, itself, was increasing all over the country and why was that, he thought. Because transportation was the key to the future of America.

CHAPTER 3

Mario understood that people could not and would not ever become wealthy through self-sufficiency. Although it was a lovely pipedream to be self-sufficient in all areas of one's life, it would not bestow wealth upon anyone. The foundation of wealth was trade and Mario knew it. For trade to be effective, there would need to be effective transportation. He knew they couldn't effectively run the restaurants without the deliveries of produce, meat, and everything else that was a restaurant's lifeblood. As soul destroying as the sudden deaths of the women in his family was, it caused him to focus, and even obsess about vehicular transportation. That obsession eventually blossomed into his vision of forming an interstate trucking company. When he was able to envisage clearly what he wanted he pled his case to Amanda and she acquiesced. He sold the store his father had established, borrowed some money, bought a truck and Palmer Transport was born.

Mario did the driving the first couple of years as Amanda was well in control of the restaurant. One truck led to two, two led to four and twenty-five years later, Palmer Transport had become the nation's largest trucking chain. Along the way, Mario was enticed into the import business and his goods of choice were Italian shoes. The inspiration came to him during a family vacation in Italy. He was feeling the pull of his heritage and the memory of his father's work ethic when Amanda announced she needed a new pair of shoes. When Mario realized how much cheaper the shoes were in Italy he conceived his idea right then and there.

Sioux Falls, South Dakota was a long way from New York both in terms of distance and activity. After her divorce in 1976 Deborah Dececchi took her fifteen-year-old son, Dino, halfway across the country for a new start. Money was no concern for her, as it had been for her father in the early years. So she was free to go wherever she wished. She reasoned that even a terrible choice could easily be remedied with wealth. She and Dino sat together one Saturday afternoon with a map of the country and began their makeshift game of relocation lottery.

Dino was a map lover ever since he got his first one at the age of three. It was no problem locating a big map, he had dozens. Political maps, relief maps, historical maps. You name it, he had it. They used a large wall map with brightly colored states shown in red, blue, green, yellow and orange. It was placed on the big cherry dining table. With a black magic marker Dino began numbering the states on the map, while his mother used a red marker to mark fifty playing cards from 1 to 50. Dino marked Alaska as number one on the map and Hawaii as number two. All the rest were marked in sequence from number three, which was Washington, to number fifty, which was Florida. Dino shuffled the cards about 113 times before they started cutting the deck, first he, and then Deborah. He also shuffled the cards for a full 20 seconds between each cut. One by one states were eliminated until just three were left; South Dakota, Maine and Alaska. To huge sighs of relief, South Dakota and Maine survived the penultimate cut. The last two cards on the table were separated and Dino turned one over. He turned over number fifteen, which was South Dakota, leaving number eleven, Maine, as the winner but Dino decided to change the rules on the last cut, because he liked the sound of South Dakota better. So did Deborah and off they went, heading west.

Fourteen years on the road hadn't soured Murray Kasic at all. He still loved to drive. In all those years he had probably seen almost every little town in the US and Canada worth looking at and even some that weren't. This life suited him, he thought. If scouting wasn't in his blood in the beginning, it certainly was by then. Who would have thought that the simple act of docking his boat on a lake in cottage country would cost him his career? His knee was cooked, that was for sure, but life continued anyway.

Murray had oftentimes expressed the view, after his boating accident, that what a person became was a direct result of what that person thought. And, in life, what a person got was a direct result of what that person gave. This philosophy of his was entrenched in his soul. It gave him great comfort. Murray probably could have become a priest had he not become involved with sports. But this was his life, and he enjoyed it immensely. Everyone who knew him well, liked him a lot. He always looked on the bright side and inspired all whose lives he touched.

This particular day, he was on his way to visit some friends in Fort Worth. He had just watched a couple of players he had his eye on at the University of Minnesota. Now it was time for a few days off so he began his meander south. Between Mountain Lake and Windom he spotted a silver Mercedes pulled off on the shoulder with the trunk lid open. A woman was half buried in it, jack at her feet. Murray thought about stopping to help, thought the better of it, and then stopped anyway. He pulled over about a hundred feet or so ahead of the stopped vehicle. As he was approaching the front of the car he called out and asked if she needed any help. An attractive, dark-haired, olive skinned woman, about his age he thought, tilted her head around the trunk lid. Murray really liked what he saw.

"I could use some help. Thanks," she said.

"You don't see too many of these at the side of the road," Murray commented.

"First time I've ever had a flat," she told him.

"Well, we'll have you goin' in no time."

"That's great. I really appreciate it."

"No problem," he told her.

It took him about fifteen minutes to change the tire and get everything back into the trunk. They made a little small talk during that time, and Murray was quite impressed with this woman. She was obviously very well off. Just how well off, he wasn't sure, but judging by the car, clothes, jewelry, deportment and bearing of this striking woman, she was well out of his league.

For her part, Deborah Dececchi was also enamored with this gentleman Samaritan. She thought his appearance and behavior were that of a centered, quiet, peaceful man. He was the kind of man she wished she had been attracted to when she was younger. Perhaps her life might have unfolded differently if she had matured a little earlier, she thought.

"So, where're you headed, Murray?"

"Fort Worth. Got a few days off. Going to visit some friends," Murray answered.

"I see. What do you do?" Deborah inquired.

"I'm a scout............ a hockey scout."

"Really? I'm just on my way back from a hockey game."

"Really? Where?"

"Minneapolis. My son plays for the Gophers," she said.

"No kidding. I just came from there myself," Murray told her.

"Yeah? Looking at anyone in particular?" Deborah's interest was piqued.

"Terry Paulson."

"Oh, yes, he is the star," Deborah proclaimed emphatically.

"What's your son's name?"

"Dino Dececchi. Number........." Deborah was halted.

"24. He's got some talent, honestly," Murray said.

"Seriously, you think so?"

"Definitely. As a freshman he's very impressive. As long as he keeps improving, who knows?" said Murray.

"That's really nice to hear. I just want him to get his MBA and get into the business. But, let's face it, he'd love to turn pro and I have to admit, I'd love it too."

"It can happen. You never know," Murray encouraged her.

"Boy, wait till I tell him what you said."

"Listen, why don't I give you my card? Tell him he can call me anytime he wants."

"I guarantee he'll call you," Deborah said.

"Good. I like talkin' to the young guys," Murray admitted.

Now that the ice was broken, so to speak, they were both energized and the conversation turned to the two of them. Quick histories preceded long gazes and smiles followed nods. There was no doubt about it. A current was moving them. They didn't acknowledge it, yet they couldn't resist it and they didn't want to.

"Now that I've got your card, can I call you too?" Deborah asked.

"Uh, yeah. I'd really like to talk to you again Deborah."

"Good," she effervesced.

"Okay, then. I'll be talkin' to you," Murray beamed.

"Take care, Murray."

"You too."

As Murray drove away, he lamented that he didn't ask for her phone number but that really would have been an awkward situation for him. Besides, she had his card and if she liked him enough she'd call him sooner or later. He began to wonder if, maybe, she was married. He finally concluded, as he merged onto the interstate, heading west, she probably wasn't married but that was her problem anyway. He berated himself for not finding out where she was going or where she lived. Or what she was talking about when she referred to the business.

Later, past Omaha, he mused about life's coincidences. He didn't believe in coincidences. He felt the only thing coincidences coincided with was destiny or fate or whatever anyone wanted to call it. He strongly believed that people create their own destiny and their own future out of their own thoughts and actions. There were always choices to be made and paths to be followed. Why had he taken a circuitous route to Fort Worth? It wasn't a huge detour that he made but he could have traveled straight down from Minneapolis. But he hadn't. A whim took him west and a woman took him aback. To Murray, thoughts were things and thoughts became things. A chair didn't exist until someone thought it into being. Likewise, with art, literature, medicine, law, architecture, or human situations, he thought. In the case of situations, Murray believed that these things, which were thoughts, became or evolved into actions, which created results, and presto, a future was created, soon to become a reality. His credo was, we are what we chose to be and we'll become what we choose to be.

Caught between what he had chosen to be and what he would choose to be, Henry had only one choice to make. That he would emerge from the dusk was a given, but would his shadow follow him out or swallow him up?

CHAPTER 4

It was already too late to erase the artificial histories he created for his own benefit, but he could've stopped there if he had wanted. Certainly, he was not the first applicant in history to embellish his credentials. People did that sort of thing all the time. Exaggerate a little, lie a little, if it got the job, what difference did it really make? As long as he was competent and capable of performing the task at hand it didn't matter to him. In the long run nobody was going to be disadvantaged by his actions, he thought. Or, at least, nobody would know.

Henry revised his history to devise his future. He saw himself giving up his private practice eventually. Envisioning a career as a sports psychologist he predicted to himself that other sports would also benefit from his expertise. Writing and lecturing would follow as surely as fame and fortune. He clearly visualized becoming an icon of sorts, a performance guru of great repute, and in great demand. And, if his newly fabricated fantasy made him very wealthy too, he wouldn't need to worry about the 'Charlene' factor. His own wealth would afford him the luxury of continuing to live alone.

He always felt that Charlene was perfect for him, so long as she was useful. Her main attribute, as Henry saw it, was in providing him the cover of normality. Being from a wealthy family came in as a close second place, only in so far as he required her presence in the first place. Now, in his daydream, he foresaw many potential scenarios in which she would no longer be an asset. When assets became liabilities there was no accounting for his loss of control.

Understanding himself very well only served to make him more elusive. He wasn't sure at what point in his past the single flash of clarity made him aware of what he really was, but it had come and gone quickly. It wasn't the sort of self realization that anyone would want to dwell on, let alone Henry. He saw his psychopathy clearly. He was called a sociopath, formerly referred to as a psychopath. At that time, he would have been labeled an antisocial personality, but he did not believe it. Whichever way his condition was expressed he was, to be sure, expressly unconditioned. He knew from his earlier epiphany that no amount of well-intentioned sensitivity or moral teaching would ever influence him. He was the Elliott Ness of psychologists. He was untouchable because he acquired the one thing that most of his ilk had not. He developed self-restraint in his demeanor, actions and oral expression. He could never be diagnosed as a psychopath if his symptoms were those of a neurotic. So he was always careful to act agitated and nervous at times, even though he was truly calm and unruffled. He was a god unto himself. His endgame was always the same, that his will, alone, be done. Shakespeare wrote that all the world's a stage and all the people merely players. To Henry, these words were more powerful than any others in the English language and their actualization, to him, was the Holy Grail itself.

As far as Charlene was concerned, he still needed her. As with most people his fantasies always played out with himself as the ultimate and unquestioned hero. But he needed the tacit approval of Charlene to implement his plans properly. She would be an unwitting accomplice to Henry. Most psychologists were not sanctioned to write prescriptions but Louisiana law had been changed to allow psychologists to write scripts if, and only if, they consulted with a psychiatrist and obtained approval to do so. So she would remain with Henry for a while. Charlene was indispensable, and without her unconscious complicity, so were the drugs.

Henry embarked on his NFL immersion weekend with great resolve. But by the end of it he was rapidly approaching his gag threshold for all things football. He was amused at the players, coaches, owners and analysts. They truly believed that what they did was of some implicit importance to society at large. Could they not see that it was just a game, he thought. It was a big business too, but it was completely predicated on fabricated competition to be the best at something meaningless, except to those involved or entranced. Was that not, though, the very basis of Henry's life? And didn't everyone do the same? Ascribing importance to something which was otherwise meaningless was the sad lot of so very many. In this regard he thought that his insularity gave him immunity but it just allowed him to function with impunity.

His feelings of immense superiority to everyone, unbeknownst to him, were spawned in the fetid waters of his own cerebral cesspool. At his core, he didn't have the confidence or the capability to openly engage or compete with people. He knew that, but could not face it. This was part of the reason that he never, ever showed his hand to anyone. His key to victory was simple. He always played by his rules, even and especially,

The Skater

while appearing to play someone else's game. He was competitor, referee, rule maker and audience to his own ability. He was God. He was more than God, he was Henry Collier.

The foggy prism through which he viewed life failed to reflect the light of reality back into the darkness of his soul. He could not see the way others saw. His myopia prevented him from realizing that it was he who had the problem. It was not just this new venture with professional sports that irked him. He felt imperious, aloof, and above the mainstream endeavors of the masses. In all of this, however, he failed to feel his intense separateness. And that, of course, was the source of the power that fueled him.

Whether hearing a symphony or watching a movie, he could never surrender completely to anything outside himself. It was not that he didn't enjoy the feelings the stimulus gave him. He was just constitutionally incapable of appreciating the value of others. He saw no one as having more intelligence, cunning or creativity than he had. Any potential rival was summarily dismissed or, more often than not, repudiated, disgraced or humiliated. These tactics allowed him to maintain his feelings of self-worth.

Desperate to be an icon himself, he vented his frustration by mentally dismantling the entire concept of iconology. While he may have been right about all the evidence of hypnosis in life, he was blind to his own. He loved nothing more than talking late into the night, with plenty of alcohol, one willing and subservient protégé and absolutely no interruptions. Even at times when he knew what he was espousing was factually incorrect or, just nonsense, it didn't matter to him. It was the adulation and worship of the acolyte that gave him life. When there were only two people in the room he was always the most important, powerful and intelligent. If he was not, he would somehow make it so. No wonder he was an emaciated looking man. The energy he expended in psychic domination was enormous.

To sit in an audience and be entertained created a peculiar circumstance for Henry. The crowd had gathered for its fix and the entertainer had appeared for his. He knew that what he was witnessing was a two-way thoroughfare of addiction. The entertainer was as addicted to the adulation as the audience was to the entertainer. The entertainer, however, was a singularity and the audience was just a random collection of distraction junkies. Therefore, the performer held sway just as Henry did. And while he seemed more aligned with the person on stage, that person did not have his insight. The artist held no sway over him.

These beliefs shaped and molded him. In any other crucible they would have been held and used judiciously. But in the confines of Henry's mind the law was written, and he had written it. His world had no color, not because he had painted it so, but because his palette had been dry since birth.

CHAPTER 5

Cameron Timchuk and Dianne Black were up-and-coming Olympic athletes when their paths fleetingly crossed Henry's. Dianne was Canada's number six ranked downhill skier and Cameron was on the precipice of figure skating stardom. They knew and saw each other on a few occasions, but were formally introduced on the evening of a CBC gala event, after which they were involved in a small fender bender. Cameron's knee was quite swollen, and Dianne felt he should have it checked out. Cameron agreed.

Henry was not the doctor on call, because Henry was not a medical doctor. He was interning at the hospital, so he told people. In fact, he was just volunteering, but he managed to find a white coat and looked sympathetic. He happened to see the two enter. The blonde woman grabbed a wheelchair and wheeled it back into the vestibule area. The darker looking man sat down in it. He was in obvious pain. Only because Henry was struck with Dianne's unkempt, yet striking beauty did he engage the two of them. Later, he learned who they were and thus, by sheer happenstance began compiling their profiles.

It was easy work, enjoyable work. He had a flair for this kind of thing. As long as the end was to deceive the method was most heartening to him. Had he been doing something honorable it would have been done in his normal state of emotional flatline. But his glee could not be restrained at times like these. To him, the only wasted time was time spent in the pursuit of good. Needless to say, he didn't waste much time.

Less than three hours after Henry started weaving his web of Web lies everything was completed. He regretted that he didn't have the time or the means to construct video footage of some kind. He didn't regret anything in the normal sense of the word. It was more of a fleeting moment of recognition that sometimes the perfect outcome was out of his reach. In any case, the 'fan club' websites with all their attendant data, statistics and links were built and would certainly pass muster on a cursory inspection. He didn't expect anyone in the Jaguar organization to invest too much time or energy in properly vetting him anyway. People believed what they wanted to believe. And this organization wanted to believe in a performance messiah to help them. He would give them the faith they sought. They wished for better performances, more productive seasons and playoff victories. He would make them wishers of men.

He couldn't have planned it better. Dianne Black was murdered while on vacation in Mexico a few years earlier, which meant that her trail would not be pursued. Cameron Timchuk suffered a series of knee injuries and the humiliation of a public gay sex scandal. He disappeared off the face of the earth, it seemed to Henry. Just as well, he thought. However, it was rumored that his present domicile was somewhere between St. Lawrence market and Lake Ontario, under the Gardiner Expressway. A skating squeegee kid. That was perfect for Henry.

He was satisfied that all the loose ends were tied up, and for one of the very few times in his life, he actually, but only momentarily, considered that there was a higher power. That he held this fleeting belief in something divine working in concert with him was surely evidence of his delusional state of mind. Or was he indeed feeling a presence? Was he cooperating with a malevolent presence or misinterpreting a good one? It didn't matter because his soul expressed itself the way it always had, stealthily, covertly and deviously. That was his path to pleasure his entire life and he saw no reason to change course.

"Excuse me, Deborah, do you have a minute? Hey Murray," Duncan Chambers, VP of football operations, said.

"Yeah, sure, come on in Duncan," Deborah Dececchi said.

"Here's the shortlist of the psychologists we compiled. You said you wanted to see it," Duncan said.

Duncan Chambers was an ex professional himself, who, like so many others in the sport, spent many years with many different organizations, working his way up the ladder. He didn't see the need to hire another doctor for an already large medical staff. Especially, when they already employed a clinical neuropsychologist.

Deborah, perusing the list, looked pensive. "Thanks. Five men? Is that it? How short was the long list?"

"Here it is here. Eleven," Duncan responded.

"And how did you arrive at five?" she asked.

"Well, three turned us down right away, one was a late refusal and the other two didn't get back to us."

"And one was a woman?"

The Skater

"Yes. Charlene Kempf-Klassen. She's a psychiatrist in Shreveport. Good credentials too," he said.

"What was her problem?" Deborah wanted to know.

"Too busy. Hospital and private practice. The usual stuff, committed to the patients she already has."

"And the others?"

"Pretty much the same deal with the other two. No time, no real interest. And let's be honest, they don't all have a track record in sports. At least, nothin' to hang your hat on."

"Okay. What about our five finalists?"

"They all seemed pretty well experienced in the sports field. Some baseball too, minors mostly. But they're well recommended," Duncan had a little resentment in his voice.

"Duncan, I know you see this as a waste of time with Dr. Bravo already here, but he's stretched quite thin, and he can't commit any more time to us."

"I know. I'm just lookin' at the size of our staff already, the bottom line."

"Well, that's what I pay you for, but it's an investment that might pay off big time. I've got a hunch," Deborah said.

"You got me there, I guess. Hunches 'r' us."

"Yeah, something like that," Deborah chuckled.

They spoke for a few more minutes bringing Murray into the conversation as well. Murray didn't say too much when Deborah was talking business. Usually, he stayed well away from the business side of things. He only came to her office to take her to lunch.

"Well, I gotta get back to my office Deborah," Duncan said.

"Alright. Thanks Duncan."

Duncan looked at Murray. "Enjoy your lunch."

"Don't worry, I will," Murray said.

Duncan turned and started to leave but was halted by Deborah. "Duncan, this original list has twelve names on it. Who's this twelfth guy?"

"Oh, that's a doctor over in Baton Rouge. Henry Collier. He wasn't even on our list, but that lady shrink in Shreveport suggested we interview him. Said she worked with him a lot."

"And?"

"Well, we did a rethink on this guy. He did call back to confirm for an interview but we told him we changed our minds, that we were lookin' for someone with more US experience."

"What do you mean?" Deborah was a bit perplexed.

"Well, the man's a Canadian expatriate. No offense, Murray."

"None taken," Murray couldn't have cared less.

"So, Henry Collier's a Canadian. Why is that a problem?" Deborah demanded.

"Truth, he sounded too eager from the get-go, according to Cal. He just didn't get a good feeling from this guy."

"Well, you know our Cal, a commie under every bed," Deborah laughed.

"Yeah, well, he said he didn't sound too mature. Said he sounded kind of squirrelly."

"And, what, that would be one step up from weaselly?"

"Yeah, I guess. Cal's got his own grading system," Duncan told her.

"Did you do a background check on him?"

"Cal started, but lost interest when he figured, why trace this guy all the way from northern Ontario when he didn't think he was the right material anyway?"

"That's two strikes, Murray," Deborah chided.

"Yeah. If you don't mind me asking, whereabouts in northern Ontario?" Murray asked Duncan.

"Some place called Temagami."

"You think you know him?" Deborah asked.

"Deb, you remember a long time ago I told you about the best damn hockey player I ever scouted?" Murray asked her.

"Yeah, Johnny..... something, right?

"That's right. Johnny Collier, from Temagami."

"Coincidence?" she quipped.

"Not likely. Temagami's just a little place. Johnny Collier got married and had a kid, I think. Moved to Niagara Falls, if I remember right."

"St. Catharines?" Duncan wondered, looking at Murray.

"That's it. I kept some tabs on him for awhile but he quit playing. Shame," Murray said.

Deborah looked at Murray and for a moment thought she saw the same younger man she had seen at the side of the road all those years ago. "So you think he could be his son?"

"Could be. I don't know. Forget I asked."

"Duncan, call him back. Find out if it's him. If it is, bring him in for an interview," she said.

"Another hunch?" Duncan smiled.

"Maybe. Murray, what do you think?"

"Well, it's none of my business. But if he is Johnny Collier's kid he's got to be good at something," Murray finished.

Henry was not pleased. The arsenal of invective leveled at the Jaguar organization fouled the air, but only until he got the second call from Duncan. Henry was really good at being, or rather appearing to be, obsequious. In fact, appearing to be something was all he was. His sense of being was only appearing to be. Never did he show what he was, only what he wanted to appear to be. He was thrown off guard when he was asked about his father. Why the hell would they care if his father was a has been, never was, hockey player? He reckoned they must have done their homework. He wondered if they had already seen his Web handiwork. It didn't matter to him now. He was going to take his shot and he wouldn't miss.

CHAPTER 6

Charlene Kempf-Klassen was a fortunate woman in that she was born into privilege. Her refinement was the result of all the benefits money could buy. She was privately schooled, individually tutored and publicly protected. Her parents, Gerry Kempf Junior and Wilhelmina Klassen were very careful to shield her from public scrutiny during her formative years. Charlene felt, when she was younger, that she was disadvantaged by her parents protectiveness. But now that she was well into her thirties her perspective had changed. She realized and was very grateful for their foresight and discipline. She credited them, entirely, for her own ambition and discipline.

Ambition without discipline, she thought, would always lead to frustration and failure because an undisciplined person cannot commit to the hard work necessary for ambition's fulfillment. Conversely, she thought discipline without ambition, would become an end in itself and with no goal beyond its mundane regimentation would cause a spiritual and emotional atrophy. In her personal view, one without the other would inevitably lead to psychological stress and perhaps worse. She had seen many suffering people who simply lacked, she thought, one of these two very basic ingredients for personal growth. She believed the ambition to get somewhere was dependent on the discipline to keep traveling the path to get there.

These beliefs of hers were partially responsible for her enamorment with Henry. She saw him as a very disciplined, goal oriented individual. After all, he overcame an abusive childhood, to excel scholastically and flourish professionally. Sure, he told her lies about his mother but, she felt, he was trying to keep Charlene's image of her as pristine as possible. And who would want to admit that his mother was a prostitute and all else that accompanied that lifestyle? No one, she concluded. If she had been shown the evidence she would have vehemently denied being an enabler for Henry. And she might well have been correct. She didn't know what he was doing. So, how could she be accused of enabling?

This was part of Henry's magic, to outwit the unwitting enabler. Through his deft disabling of her conscious ability to see him for what he was, he made her an accomplice unaware. Henry out-anticipated another opponent but Charlene never considered herself an opponent of his. Why would she consider someone she loved an adversary? Only because her secret adversary cared nothing for her. Her ignorance was much more important to him than her love.

She was not the only one who was ignorant. Henry didn't know that, were it not for Charlene's mention of his name to the Jaguars staff, he wouldn't even have been considered for the opportunity he coveted. Was ignorance bliss? It certainly was for him.

"Hello," Henry said, picking up the phone.

"Hi, Henry. It's me, how are you?" Charlene asked him.

"Excellent. You?"

"Great. So what's happening with the Jags?"

"Everything's on course. Jeannie's rescheduling appointments now. Thursday's the day," Henry could barely contain himself.

"Good. Want some company?"

"What do you mean? On Thursday?"

"Yeah, why not? I'll take the day off," Charlene excitedly said.

It was at moments like these that Henry really was effortlessly callous. She might be hurt by what he was going to say but he was going to say it anyway. He found that in relationships his partners always managed to become invasive. And he deeply resented it.

"Sorry, Char. I never thought you'd want to go with me. So I chartered a fishing boat for the afternoon."

"By yourself?" Charlene was incredulous.

"I sure as hell hope not. I'm planning to take some of the Jaguar people with me."

"Henry, you don't really expect them to tell you right away if they want to retain you, do you?"

"Probably not," Henry admitted.

"Then why....?" she was cut off by Henry.

"Because it makes me look like I'm not just there for them. And don't worry, I'll get somebody to go out with me."

"You're too much," she said.

"Yeah, I am. Listen, I have to go, got a call. Talk to you later."

"Bye," Charlene whispered.

Henry had no intention of renting a fishing boat or taking anyone from the Jaguar organization out on the water. He knew how pretentious and transparently weak he would have looked. He just didn't want Charlene anywhere near Jacksonville while he was there. He didn't like to have his style cramped. He planned to have a little R&R, and that didn't include any woman he already knew. He always preferred sex with newbies, preferably bought and paid for, discreetly, whatever the cost. Priceless, he thought.

His quirky predilection for women with uneven and dissimilar nostrils was something that only a handful of escort services in the country could accommodate. When coupled with his request for elongated, unpierced earlobes the list of compliant agencies grew even smaller. But there was one escort service in Florida capable of meeting his eccentric and rather creepy needs. He used this agency whenever he had the opportunity.

Even as a psychologist he found himself perplexed as to how this bizarre fetish of his came to be. He reckoned that if he had used some self-psychotherapy techniques he could have succeeded in unearthing the cause. But he knew that if he did so he would surely remove most, if not all, of the arousing hypnotic effects of his strange facial fetish. He would never punish himself by removing a pleasure source. Henry was not the type of person to joke, at least for real, but he did once joke to himself that, perhaps as a youngster, he became infatuated with a female ear nose and throat doctor.

Jon Buchanan was a sports reporter with the Florida Times-Union. A Floridian by birth, his life took a long roundabout route to deliver him back to his home state. Jon's father was a staff sergeant in the U.S. Air Force and Jon, of necessity, had lived in six different states and Germany during his stable but nomadic upbringing. He was not averse to planting roots, but he still relished being on the move. This was why, when any new professional opportunity presented itself, he would usually take it. Working for the Florida Times-Union was one of those opportunities. It also gave him the chance of furthering his desire to freelance for various sports magazines. He most enjoyed the stress-free atmosphere in which he could pursue his story of choice, since there were no deadlines to be met. This aspect further allowed him to do the real investigative work he enjoyed so much.

His favorite pastime growing up was watching investigative crime shows on TV. He found these types of programs, both fictional and nonfictional, quite riveting. The very idea that the police detectives could backtrack from a crime scene and construct, from beginning to end, the motive and method of criminal acts was very interesting and exciting to him. He fantasized that he was the tough and grizzled looking detective, whose sworn duty it was to catch the bad guy, elicit a confession and put the criminal away.

As Jon matured, he began reading whodunits and stories and books about true crimes. It was during this enlightened period of reading that he first began to think about the writers who wrote those accounts. It seemed to him that they must have had just as much satisfaction as the cops about whom they wrote. He eventually came to the conclusion that reporting on events held its own mystique. The reporter got to experience the story from every possible angle and perspective. The reporter could live vicariously through all the characters, from the cops to the criminals to the victims. He knew from early on that a reporter had the power to influence public opinion, but also the responsibility to report without prejudice.

Jon enjoyed sports almost as much as he enjoyed investigative reporting. That was precisely why he began freelancing for sports magazines. It was also the reason he got into sports reporting in the first place. He managed to get a few freelance pieces published, here and there, but those were mainly fluff pieces. What he really craved was becoming a featured writer for one of the big magazines. He also had an ambition to be a syndicated columnist. So, for the time being, his ambivalence held him captive.

He was a staunch family man, but hadn't yet created a situation to start one. He came close a few times but nothing permanent ever came of his romances. One day, he thought, he'd find the right woman and settle down to start a family. Until then, he wasn't looking. He was just aware and receptive.

His mother died when he was thirteen and his father raised him with little help. Moving from one colorless base to another around the country and from one sterile military housing enclave to another was something Jon endured. Even though friends were always left behind, he stoically accepted that all the other kids lived the same life. And that was just the way it was. He made friends easily and probably as a result of his life as the son of a military man, he always would. Whenever he was asked why he never enlisted in the military himself, his reply was always the same. "I already spent eighteen years in the Air Force. Why would I want to do it again?"

Jon's father, Winston Buchanan, left Mississippi to join the U.S. Air Force in 1979 during the Iran hostage crisis. Doing patriotic service seemed to blend well with his desire to create a better life for himself and his expanding family. They both felt the urge to change their lives before the baby was born, because after Jon's arrival, they would find many reasons not to do it.

Winston and Sherry were a couple with a deep sense of family values. They were semireligious, but wholly spiritual and their faith in God grew with each new blessing received. They were ever grateful for what they had, each other, their son and their bountiful life and boundless freedom to watch Jon grow and to participate in his daily joy of discovery. In their pursuit of happiness they were overtaken by fulfillment. Meaning replaced searching and gratitude transformed want.

This was the atmosphere into which Jon was born and raised. Steeped as he was in this loving and thankful environment, it was no wonder that he thrived. In natural fashion, his character evolved more through psychic osmosis than reward and punishment. He was a thoroughly good boy and was destined to become an even better man. He never found doing the right thing difficult. If the consequences were difficult, then that hardship was as necessary as bad tidings from a poor decision. Jon didn't concern himself with outcomes. He preferred to focus his energy on his intent, which was to act honestly and morally without obsessive regard for the future, which he believed would take care of itself. And it usually did.

It was mid-June when Jon first heard about the Jaguar's interest in hiring a 'performance specialist'. He sure didn't see much wrong with the idea, considering their abysmal collapse in the last half of the previous season. Anyway, he thought it would give him some pretty good copy throughout the season. He planned to get at least one interview with whomever was hired. He felt he might be able to develop an in-depth article on the subject.

PROFESSIONAL SHRINKAGE by Jon Buchanan

Whenever a professional football team takes the field it's the result of thousands of collective hours of work and preparation. This year's Jaguars are certain to be not only well-prepared and well coached but well shrunk too. Before you think they've all been on low carbohydrate diets, please let me clarify.

The team is in the process now of interviewing six 'performance specialists' for a newly created position. The successful candidate will work under the direction of team physician, Dr. Cal Heinbecker, and clinical neuropsychologist, Dr. Osvaldo Bravo.

No one has admitted it, but last year's implosion in November and December seems to be the driving force behind this decision. Outscored by an average of nineteen points a game the last half of last season, it's not surprising that management felt a need to do something. Anything. Talk about a 'brains trust'. No names have been released yet.

CHAPTER 7

Henry wore his newest and most expensive dark blue suit with a $300 shirt and a $200 red power tie. His medium length dark brown hair was cut to a longish short, and his black Italian shoes, with lifts, were shining with such brilliance that they might have lit up a black hole in space. He carried with him a thin black briefcase, which contained his resume and the false document. He typed the false document, as it turned out. He changed his mind about handwriting his supposed work with the two athletes. After all, for a job this specific how could he almost forget to list the appropriate experience?

Calvin Heinbecker was a large man. He weighed about two hundred sixty pounds and stood about six foot four. He was still in pretty decent condition, even though he was fast approaching sixty. His hair was short and gray with a small bald spot at his crown. But to his credit, he made no attempt to hide it. He was robust with rosy cheeks, and still pretty darned good teeth. He looked relaxed and well-dressed in a half casual suit, half sweats kind of way. In fact, he could have worn a clean white T-shirt and have looked almost formally attired.

"Henry," Cal said, as Henry rose from his chair.

"Mr Heinbecker," Henry replied, hand outstretched.

"Please, call me Cal."

"Okay, Cal. Very nice to meet you."

"And you, Henry. Please come into my office. Have a seat."

As both men seated themselves, each one began to formalize his opinion of the other. Neither opinion was complimentary. Cal's first impression was that Henry was very nervous and, as he surmised during the phone call, devious too. Henry initially thought that Cal was a lot like his own father. He liked to softly intimidate people with his physical presence. Henry saw and felt that Cal didn't like him. Good, he thought. Cal, on the other hand, expected Henry to fold like the nervous little gnat he was. One of them was wrong.

Henry knew he would need to be very subtle with this man. He would entirely skip any effort to achieve some rapport with him, because he would know what he was trying to do. And Henry assumed, correctly, that all the others would certainly have done so. He wanted to exploit Cal's immediate dislike for him. He also realized the team physician probably wouldn't have the final say on his hiring. Henry determined that he would have a lot of input, but the final decision would rest with someone higher up the food chain.

"Henry, would you like a coffee?"

"Yes, that would be nice. Thank you."

"Tommy, can you bring some coffee in for me and Henry please?" Cal shouted around the open door. "We'll get started once the coffee gets here, Henry. If you'll pardon me for just a moment I've just got to write a script before I forget. Please, relax."

"Certainly," Henry said.

As Cal went about pulling prescription pads out of his oak desk drawer and rummaging through papers on top of the desk, Henry looked around the office. Football photographs were everywhere. Some were old and some were new. The newer ones featured the Jaguars in one way or another, while the older ones showed Cal Heinbecker in his more youthful days. Cal attended Oklahoma State and played tight end for the Sooners until a fractured femur ended his playing career. That was when he decided to become a doctor. But, of course, Henry knew all this, having already researched the physician.

He also knew the ruse about the prescription and waiting for the coffee was just Cal's clumsy and amateurish way of trying to disrupt him. Henry had planned to use all manner of psychological ploys to gain the upper hand in this interview. But he knew he would have to pick his spots carefully. He considered, only for a fleeting moment, that maybe Cal was baiting him. He overruled that idea immediately. He was sure Cal had already made up his mind about him. He felt the good doctor was poised to rid himself of him in short order. Henry was aware that any successful applicant would surely have another interview to contend with but Cal would decide who moved on.

"Here's the coffee Doc," Timmy said.

"Thanks Timmy. Shut the door on your way out, will you?"

"Sure."

Timmy had presented the two men with a nice-looking royal blue corning wear tray. It was jam-packed with two mugs, coffee pot, cream and sugars, sweeteners, stir sticks and biscotti. Cal poured coffee into the mugs and gestured Henry to customize his as he wished. Henry did as instructed, slowly and deliberately, giving Cal time to prepare his as well. Henry bit half into a biscotti and ate it ravenously. Quickly thereafter he snorted the other half. Cal put a little cream and one sweetener into his cup as he furtively glanced at Henry, who chomped on a second biscotti like a beaver on a conifer. He then proceeded to pour too much cream into his coffee, followed rhythmically by seven sugars, ripping them up like spent betting slips.

If Cal hadn't disliked him so much he would have laughed. But all he could think of was how thoroughly uncouth Henry was. He was thinking of his belief that skinny people seem to be able to eat anything they want. Seven sugars, that was ridiculous. And he'd better hurry up and grab a biscotti before the little shrew took them all.

"How is the biscotti?" asked Cal.

"Good, thanks. I haven't had anything since breakfast," Henry said.

"What time was that?"

"Eight thirty. IHOP."

"IHOP?" Cal asked, noting that eight thirty was only two hours ago.

"Yeah, I always have a combo, omelette and pancakes, the usual."

"Really? Could've fooled me."

"Yeah, I never gain weight no matter what I eat," Henry boasted.

"What's your secret?"

"Law of attraction, actually."

"And how does that work?" Cal took the bait.

Henry was beginning to feel much more in control. He hated his coffee and actually gave up adding sugar years ago. But today, it really tasted good in a strange kind of way. He knew this big man had been fighting his weight all his life. There weren't too many things more annoying for someone of girth than to watch a thin person eat and drink with impunity.

"You attract whatever you think about. If you think you're fat, you will be," Henry answered.

"You think it's that simple?" Cal, looking irritated, asked.

"I know it is, Cal. I know the mind. It is."

"There are lots of other reasons, Henry. Thyroid, diabetes onset, depression, improper nutrition, to name a few, Cal argued.

"Of those four things, which one do you suffer from?"

"Don't have any but that's not the point."

"Then why are you fighting your weight?" Henry annoyingly asked.

"I'm not fighting it. That's why I work out. I'm a good twenty pounds over my ideal weight, I agree, but that's just age."

Cal had just told three lies and Henry knew it. It was obvious the doctor consciously held in his stomach most of the time. That was a classic sign that he was uncomfortable with his silhouette. His long sleeved T-shirt was tucked in his trousers, but a good two inches of it had been pulled up, all around his waist so that he had a midriff comfort zone to obscure his love handles and belly fat without stretching the fabric too far. The flap of material at the top of his zipper, which ran parallel to his pants waist, was stretched so that the two lines of fabric didn't form a 90° angle in the front because the circumference of his trousers waist was smaller than his own. Henry also detected an almost imperceptible crease at his belt line caused by the pressure of his stomach pushing over it. His face and neck were too large for even a man of his size, giving him that overstuffed, hog jowled, Ted Kennedy look.

"Well, I'm sure you didn't bring me here to discuss your weight problems," Henry snipped.

"Indeed!" He wondered why in hell he was even entertaining this little twerp. Oh yeah, Murray and Deborah wanted him in the mix. Two things were obvious to Cal. Henry probably shaved with a Kleenex and wiped his ass with a Q-tip. "Okay, Henry, why should we hire you? What can you offer this organization that would make us want to bring you on board?"

"One, I'm a winner. I win. I don't lose. You're a team that loses. You don't win. I am also capable of making individuals winners so your team can and will win. Not hiring me, Cal, is just more evidence of your losing ways."

"No. You're wrong. Not hiring anyone would be proof of that. Not hiring you would just be a business decision," Cal told him.

Henry admitted to himself that Cal's rejoinder was a pretty good one. But rather than fight him on it he would let him think the point was conceded, and move on. "Point taken."

Cal Heinbecker proceeded to move the interview in an orderly direction. He started with Henry's credentials, and then moved to his experience and successes. He grudgingly conceded that Henry was qualified, but that didn't make him any more appealing. He'd rather have suffered hemorrhoids than Henry, because at least when the hemorrhoids were gone the asshole wouldn't bother you anymore. He explained to Henry that selected players would consult with whomever was hired. It would depend, he said, on their performances or problems affecting their play. He also told him that he could be consulting with different players during different weeks.

"What about follow-up consultations?" Henry asked.

"Of course, that'll happen as necessary," Cal answered.

Henry told him he foresaw a serious problem with scheduling. There could be a dozen or more players who needed follow-up sessions, he said. He wanted to know, as well, if any players had the autonomy to see him

The Skater

even if they were not directed to do so by management. Of course they would, Cal told him, but that would be on their own dime. The Jaguars were not going to pay for player initiated private consultations.

"You shouldn't need to see too many players anyway," Cal said.

"Oh, really? Have you seen them play?" Henry chirped.

That last shot totally pissed off Cal. Who did this runt think he was? Baiting Henry now, Cal turned the conversation back to medical issues. He mentioned that Henry, because he was not a medical doctor, would need him to write any necessary prescriptions. If he was hired, of course. The old Sooner had decided to start turning the screw.

"If I'm hired, of course, I'll write my own scripts," Henry snapped.

"You're not an M.D. You can't," Cal almost shouted.

"I'm not an M.D. but I certainly can. It's Louisiana law. I'm licensed in Louisiana. I can write my own, Cal. Check it out," Henry jabbed.

Cal was taken aback and to say the least a little dumbfounded. His plan to knock him down a peg or two had just failed. But was this really true? He wasn't sure, but he couldn't go on the offensive without risking looking like an idiot. "Special Cajun rules?"

"Something like that," Henry said, noting that Cal had just blown his big chance to make him look foolish. Turnabout was fair play.

And so it went for a good hour and a half. First, Cal made the explanations, and then Henry clarified them. Then, Cal explained things further, followed by Henry's objections and disagreements. Cal grew more infuriated with every passing minute, and Henry could see, even feel, the tension in the big man rising. During the entire last half of the interview, Henry used a number of subtle psychological maneuvers on Cal. Every time he elucidated an answer to the doctor, he was either embedding commands, dispatching truth anchors, or just being a general irritant.

When he decided to comment on the big framed picture of Cal in his hunting regalia, things began to change. Henry told him he had never fired a gun in his life and thought, respectfully, that guns were a societal sickness. They bantered back and forth for a few minutes until Henry was ready to change the subject in order to upset Cal from a different angle. Then, it happened and Henry was delighted.

Cal began to tell him how, even though he had taken the Hippocratic oath, if anyone ever harmed his family he would have no compunction whatsoever in using that beautiful rifle in the picture. Then, he clearly outlined how he would do it and why no one would or could ever find the remains of the offender.

Henry knew precisely what Cal was doing. He was now, openly, trying to intimidate him. Henry thought that was perfect. The man's anger was just under the surface now, unmasked. The time had arrived for Henry to perform a little surgery of his own on the team physician. Like a cop setting up a criminal to force a confession, Henry used a tried and tested technique. He wanted Cal to openly admit how he felt toward him. Once that was done, Henry reasoned, Cal would be finished. Henry said, "You're an educated man, a physician, in good shape, and you're a hunter too. Tell me the truth, would you really do that?"

"You better believe it," Cal shot back.

"Don't you worry that since your well-respected, well-liked and you're held in high esteem that when you tell the truth about something like this people might balk or you'll blow your cover?" Henry asked.

"I'm only telling you, nobody else."

"So your being a doctor doesn't conflict with being a potential murderer? So, if you tell me want to hurt me and you show me how you'll do it and you scare the shit out of me, where does that lead?"

"Nowhere, it's just hypothetical, Henry."

"I know this hasn't been a fun interview for you. I'm a very difficult guy to get along with but let's face it, you already know that. I'm just an expendable job applicant, and you want to get rid of me, right?"

"Ahh." Cal breathed lethargically. "I'm really tired of this bull shit. And yeah, I do want to get rid of you. ASAP, if you don't mind."

"What would someone have to do to a family member, Cal?"

"What?"

"Would rape to do it for you? Would that make you go and get your gun?"

"You're a god damn disgrace to your profession," Cal shouted at him.

"Oh, I see! You've got homicidal fantasies, but I'm the disgrace."

"I don't have homicidal fantasies, you idiot. I don't have a malicious bone in my body," Cal was incredulous.

"Really? If that's true then you're just a malicious liar, correct?" Henry spit back.

"No. I lied, but with no malice."

"You just lied again. You can't stand me, and that means malice, or you're fabricating," Henry felt empowered.

"How did we ever let you in our country, for God's sake? You are, without a doubt, the worst candidate for a job, any job, I've ever seen. Am I ever glad you're such an asshole 'cause throwin' you out will be the most fun I've had in a long time," Cal yelled, completely exasperated.

"Would you kill me?"

"What?" Cal was losing it.

"If I, I don't know, if I anally raped your wife, would you shoot me Doc? Would you shoot me?"

"Get outta here, you sick bastard!" screamed Cal, and as he did so he pounded the desktop and accidentally hit his laptop, which crashed to the floor. Furious, he reached toward Henry as he lunged around his desk. He turned the doorknob and completely beside himself pushed Henry out the door and then slammed it shut.

Somewhere between fifteen and twenty seconds elapsed before the door was opened again. From the outside, it was Henry. He saw Cal Heinbecker, seated behind his desk, flushed, flabbergasted and looking downright disappointed with himself. He looked up at Henry, saying nothing, appearing somehow vacant.

"Well?" Henry asked.

"Well, what?" Cal asked.

"Come on. Tell me. I've got the job right?"

"Not a chance in hell."

"Really? Have you ever acted like that before? In a professional setting, conducting a serious interview? Be honest with yourself now, we only want what's best for the team. Did I or did I not, in just over ninety minutes, totally and completely change your behavior and your performance in a professional arena?" Henry taunted him.

"Piss off."

"Looking forward to working with you, Cal."

Henry didn't close the door as he minced away down the hall.

"Okay, bye." Deborah put down the phone and looked at Murray as she tried, unsuccessfully, to suppress a grin. She was proud of him for his input into the plan to hire a performance specialist. After all, he had many years of experience in professional sports. But he was only a scout, and the sport just happened to be hockey. He never felt comfortable trying to influence any decision she made with her team. He never wanted to impose his will on anyone.

"What's the smile all about?" Murray asked.

"That was Duncan. He said he just had a, what was it, a cathartic conversation with Cal about Henry Collier."

"And?"

"Seems this guy gave Cal a very difficult time. A mind game freak, that's what Cal called him. Said he's manipulative, arrogant, sneaky, and completely disingenuous. And he thinks we should hire him."

CHAPTER 8

This season was playing out very much the way everyone in the Jaguar organization envisioned it. The preseason exposed a lot of problems they had been working on but that was exactly the reason for playing the preseason schedule. They finished two and two, and that was fine with Deborah. It was more important to assess talent and gain information to improve the team than to worry about winning. There would be plenty of time to live or die by wins and losses in the regular season.

After the first eight weeks of the season their record was 6 and 2, a lot better than their dismal performance the previous year which saw them win the first six games in a row and then lose the next seven out of eight. They finished that season with an 8 and 8 record. But it was really much worse than it appeared, because they progressively worsened over the course of the season. That made three consecutive losing seasons of 7 and 9, 6 and 10, 8 and 8. It was at the end of the 6 and 10 season that Deborah Dececchi made a coaching change and brought in Dave Mann.

Dave Mann had only college experience when she hired him. What he lacked in pro experience he seemed to more than make up for in organizational skills, talent assessment, dedication and the ability to motivate players and staff alike.

It seemed to Deborah that the team's new blood was coursing rapidly through the Jaguar system. She felt confident and optimistic. This was the way the season should progress, she thought. The team was 1 and 1 after the first two games but had won the next five of five and most important hadn't lost a single game to divisional rivals. Their loss the week before resulted in a change of field-goal kickers. The placekicker missed four field goals in a row, and that wasn't the first time his performance was poor. So he was cut and replaced.

Bringing Henry into the organization was another decision of Deborah's that seemed to be paying dividends. He really did seem to be helping with some of the more volatile and unproductive players. There wasn't a solitary player in legal trouble that season except for those whose problems had followed them from the previous year. It seemed to her that even those players were much more team oriented this season. Statistically, nearly everyone on the roster was performing better than they had performed the last two years. Skeet Leach, the quarterback she had considered trading last year, had a completion percentage of sixty, and his touchdown to interception ratio was second-best in the league. Of course, one of the biggest reasons for that was the tremendous improvement of the offensive line, which was being tutored by a new line coach. It was also being tweaked by 'King Henry' as some of his protégés had dubbed him.

The strangest thing was beginning to happen in the opinion of the team physician and the coaches who shared Cal's inherent distrust of Henry. The players who consulted with Henry, to a man, loved him. It was simply a classic 'Henryesque' side effect. He did have a certain savoir faire when it came to enlisting the loyalty of bigger, stronger, but psychologically inferior people. He always was able and eager to do that. He relished it, in fact.

Henry never thought of things philosophical, because morality, if it existed at all, was an unknown concept to him. Had he been a man of substance he might have viewed certain instances in his life as watershed events; situations which presented two clear paths of forward progress. However, having no such scruples he saw no reason for even a cursory examination of his past. He lived in a sterile and vacuous world of random artificial illuminations, all destined to be cloaked by the curtain of night. Thoughts, images, memories and more disappeared quickly beneath his heavy thought horizon, never to be seen again. A memory was the mind's hypnotic side effect, for use only in eliciting desired behaviors or placating certain subjects of his. He believed a memory was nothing other than a type of selfish cerebral fixation. He said many times to many people that a trip down memory lane was just mental masturbation. Yet, he was blind to his own selfish pleasures as evidence of the same dynamic. But only because he never remembered them.

When he was seventeen years old he had a friend, actually a fairly close friend, called Alan Bean. Henry and Alan had been friends for about six years. Henry was almost a year older than Alan. But as always was the case, Henry was considerably smaller and lighter than Alan. Throughout their youth they hung around together. They played street hockey, catch in the backyard and just generally ran around the neighbourhood. The tension between them lay just under the surface. Alan was outwitted by Henry at every turn and that fueled much of the resentment that Alan felt toward him.

The Skater

The minefield of the psyche of young Alan wasn't altogether too different from those of all his friends. They worried about girls and felt nervous around girls. So desperate was Alan for female approval that he, in his fear, withdrew from normal interaction and therefore seemed aloof. Some girls, bless their hearts, saw the goodness in Alan and made tentative advances toward him. Alan was big and strong and quite good-looking, but he didn't know it. Henry made sure of that. He sabotaged Alan's burgeoning love life at every opportunity and whenever possible.

One of those incidents of sabotage was probably not too serious on the face of it. But combined with all the other little things Henry did, it certainly contributed to Alan's alcoholism and subsequent suicide at the age of nineteen. Alan's psychic minefield was never swept and Henry's malevolent use of incendiary devices finally resulted in Alan blowing his brains out on a wet Thursday morning in April. The television was on when the police arrived, in response to a neighbor's 911 call. It was tuned to a documentary, because Alan liked to learn new things and expand his mind, which of course is exactly what he did when he blew it all over the ceiling.

Brenda Downs was almost a year older than Alan. She lived across the street from the boys who lived two doors apart from each other. Alan harbored an enormous crush for Brenda. She knew it but Alan was not aware that she knew it. Henry understood exactly what was happening and nothing gave him greater pleasure than planting the seeds of doubt in both of them. Brenda was one of the girls who could see through Alan's defenses, and besides, she thought he was a real hunk. She stayed late after school sometimes in the fall to watch the football team practice. Mostly, it was Alan she was watching. Alan noticed her. Henry watched them both.

One mild, sunny day in spring the ice appeared to break between the two. Henry and Alan were walking home from the local variety store. Tossing a football back and forth as they walked, an errant pass eluded Alan and landed at the back stairs of Brenda's house. As luck would have it she was bringing in the laundry off the clothesline. She bent and picked up the ball and began playing catch with Alan. As Henry came closer, he joined in, and in his usual fashion started to direct the conversation. Henry positioned himself between them and as the throwing lanes of the football created a larger and larger triangle, he redirected the ball so that Alan threw to Brenda. He didn't want Alan receiving anything from Brenda. He knew Alan felt much more awkward throwing the ball to her than he would have felt receiving it from her. Two more wild passes from Henry and Alan was completely marginalized. On the last high and wide throw Henry closed the gap with Brenda. As Alan sprinted back, after retrieving the ball, he could see they were talking and smiling and laughing. Henry said it was time to go, so it was time to go.

The following day Henry told Alan that Brenda had asked him who the creep was. Alan, in his innocence and stupidity, at that point, wasn't even sure if Brenda knew what his name was. All those times he saw her at football practice gave him the feeling that she liked him. Now, he was convinced that she liked somebody else. He thought about how he could have been so stupid. He felt humiliated. He felt like he was a creep. Henry felt like a king.

Later that summer, Alan's parents took a trip to Florida with his younger brother. Alan stayed to work his summer job at the dairy whipping up ice cream cones and milkshakes. He would never have abused the privilege of having the house to himself, but being Henry's serf it seemed he always found himself being compromised. On the first available evening, while Alan was working until 11 PM, Henry arranged a party at Alan's house. They had arranged earlier in the day that Henry would stay over a few nights while Alan's parents were away. By the time Alan returned from work the party was well underway. He was angry but the peer pressure to save face and not appear ruffled, muted his displeasure. He acquiesced to Henry's will yet again.

About an hour later, Henry mentioned to him that Brenda was over earlier, but left because her parents wanted her home before eleven. "Oh, yeah?" Alan was still hopeful that maybe she liked him after all. His hopes would be dashed in short order.

"Yeah, she went upstairs with Tony," Henry lied.

"Oh yeah?" Alan tried to act unfazed by it, but he couldn't hide his disappointment.

"Hey, man. They wanted to go in your parent's room, but I wouldn't let 'em."

"Thanks." Henry delighted in the fact that Alan sounded deflated.

"I think they went in your room."

Alan didn't feel too well. He just wanted everyone out of his house, but he knew he'd have to wait a while because he didn't possess the courage to chuck everyone out. So he smiled and pretended that everything was all right. He knew he would have a massive cleanup to undertake in the morning and he knew he'd be doing it himself. That was just the way it was for Alan. Henry made messes. Alan cleaned them.

It was almost two in the morning before everyone finally cleared out, including Henry, who went to someone else's house. He was pleased that Henry left. He didn't actually like him. Why was he his friend anyway? He felt terribly used. He was in love with Brenda, but now all this had happened. He was feeling very tired and very depressed. He just wanted to sleep. Tomorrow was cleanup day and he had to be at work by noon. As his head hit the pillow, the back of his right thigh squeezed and squished on the used condom Henry left in his bed. Alan was doomed and Henry knew he'd never say a word about it.

CHAPTER 9

Jon Buchanan was drawing the ire of Deborah Dececchi. She was annoyed at his repeated references to 'shrinkage' in his articles. She felt Henry was performing admirably. So well, in fact, that she asked Henry to grant Buchanan an interview but he invariably seemed reluctant to the idea. She was not in any legal position to force him to be interviewed but she did try, with no luck, to convince him. His reluctance perplexed her and she was not the only one.

Jon had done his due diligence in checking into the background of his only recalcitrant Jaguar. It appeared Henry Collier had a normal upbringing, without incident. He did well in school at every level and had no criminal record. Neither privileged nor disadvantaged, he grew up in a nondescript fashion to become the first Collier to graduate from university. His subsequent emigration to Louisiana was also commonplace. There seemed nothing untoward or out of the ordinary about Henry. And yet Jon couldn't get past his gut instinct about the man he'd never met.

An idea began to gel in Jon's mind to compare what Henry was doing for the Jaguars with what he had done for those two Canadian athletes. So he sat down with a couple of players, Skeet Leach, the quarterback and Michael Jenkins, the veteran wide receiver. His plan was to soften up Henry with some very flattering reportage. Considering the great season they were having, it didn't seem too far-fetched for Jon to pen a nice feel good piece that might appeal to Henry's ego.

The quarterback and the wide receiver both spoke of Henry in glowing terms. They found him disconcerting at first but after a few meetings and a few games they began to enjoy his quirkiness. There was nothing like success to turn an athlete's opinion, Jon supposed. They explained in great detail how Henry helped them but they were both averse to divulging the style or substance of their respective consultations. It wasn't that Henry needed to remind them that everything said was said in confidence. There was no way either of these guys was going to tell anything unbecoming about himself.

Skeet told Jon about his throwing mechanics and how even though the quarterback coach did most of the tutelage, it was cemented by Henry's positive reinforcement. He went on to tell him that part of Henry's success was his lack of charm. Downright boorish was the term Skeet used to describe the doctor he would later refer to as a real friend.

Michael also waxed philosophical about Henry. He told Jon how visualization techniques helped him see the ball better and bigger. His hands, he said, thought for themselves without the aid of his mind. He was running better, more precise routes, jumping higher, and catching better. And he owed it all to Henry, he said.

The resulting article was fair, balanced and contained much of the accolades which had been bestowed upon Henry. It was penned to move him to grant an interview. But again he refused. Jon was quite frustrated, so he decided to take another tack. He'd contact the two amateur athletes to get their opinions.

There was no shortage of reports, articles and video footage of Dianne Black. Googling her quickly became an exercise in masochism. Along with the scores of websites dedicated to her skiing prowess, there were hundreds of links to the fatal shooting in Mexico. Her fiancé, initially the prime suspect, had been drugged and was apparently unconscious during the violent rape and murder. Forensics later confirmed that he could not have been involved in the crime. Unfortunately, there were no arrests and Mexican police laid no charges. The Black family, through all the legal and political means at their disposal, were unable to exert any leverage on the Mexican authorities.

Mr. Andrew Black, Dianne's father, created a citizens watchdog group to try and further bring to bear pressure on Mexican and Canadian authorities. Try as he might, like so many other grieving survivors of Mexican violence, he got absolutely nowhere. As angry as he was at the Mexican officials, he was truly livid with his own government. Eventually, he would discover that a few lives here and there were not important enough to upset the apple cart of international trade. A few platitudes, some hollow rhetoric and a meaningless government check were about all Mr. Black could count on.

After too many minutes of reading the tragedy of Dianne Black, Jon turned his attention solely to her athletic career. She was truly on the rise, and some of her fan-based websites bore out her improvements after she began to consult with Henry Collier. No doubt about it, Jon thought, she was good and Henry made her better. However, with her dead, there was

The Skater

no reason for any further follow-up. So Jon left her and her memory alone and turned to the figure skater, Cam Timchuk.

Here was an athlete who had literally suffered through his artistic and athletic skills. A unipolar depressive his entire life, he began medication in his mid-teens. According to his mother, the drugs seemed to work early in his therapy. But thereafter, they became less and less effective. As with so many depressed people, his doctor hadn't simply increased the dosage. He placed Cameron in cognitive therapy to help him think better and perceive the world in a more positive way. Nothing seemed to be of any long-lasting benefit and he underwent sporadic bouts of deep depression, which obviously affected his performance. It was his concentration that was his problem and Henry had been contracted to focus it.

According to the information on the websites and their links to newspaper articles, Henry seemed to have the gifts of Merlin at his disposal. It was reported that his work with Timchuk was as amazing as his aid had been to Dianne Black. Jon read further that Cameron had suffered some very nasty knee injuries and they plagued him until he could no longer compete. Then came the gay sex scandal, which Jon surmised, sent him over the edge of depression and hurled him headlong into outright alcoholism, from which he had not yet recovered.

Where Cam Timchuk lived after his fall from grace was anybody's guess. Jon made some attempts to locate him but he discovered, as Henry had, that Cameron was now one of the army of forgotten street people roaming the concrete and asphalt of any big city. He would have given up and let go of the idea of finding Cameron except for one thing. It was something vague in Jon's mind. He wasn't exactly sure what it was. But he followed his hunch.

Back again through all the details he searched. Everything got a second, closer scrutiny. What was he looking for? He didn't know what it was. But he knew when he found it he would know it. Was it something factual that didn't fit? No, he was certain the facts held up to examination. It was something though, he was sure, and he stayed up half the night looking. One strong hunch and his investigative mind took over. He found nothing that night, but he knew there was something. He felt it in his soul, and he was confident that eventually he would find it. Whatever it was.

The NFL commissioner's office never saw so many zany ideas for rule changes in any prior season. And they all came from the same source, Henry Collier. He mistakenly, or not at all caring, thought he could single-handedly change the game of football for the better. This was certainly not the way the league operated. A phone call to the Jaguars owner from the league commissioner should have put an end to the issue. Deborah assured the commissioner that she had not authorized any of these rule change submissions. In fact, she told him she knew nothing about them. And if her team's letterhead was used, it was definitely without her approval.

The commissioner's office faxed copies of Henry's desired rule changes to Deborah, and she then shared them with Murray before showing them to the head coach and the rest of his staff. Everyone had a great laugh at Henry's expense. In a strange way and perhaps in a parallel universe some of his ideas might have passed muster. But no one was prepared to fundamentally transform America's game.

One of his nuttier ideas was to make changes to the goalposts. No one was sure, because nobody asked him, but some of the coaches were certain he must have picked the idea up from watching Australian rules football. Goalposts, being configured like the top half of a capital H, but without the two bottom vertical lines, have a single lower vertical post in the middle of the cross post. Henry's idea was to add another four or five foot cross post on the outside of each of the two upper vertical posts. These would be six or eight feet higher than the main cross post with, of course, attached vertical posts at the ends of the two new cross posts. The result, some said, looked like a giant cactus.

His reasoning was that a missed field goal, if it went through the smaller and higher secondary goalposts, would garner the kicking team one point for field position. He was roundly teased by everyone, but he was not deterred. In fact, his very best idea was to resurrect the dropkick. The dropkick was still allowed within the rules but his idea took it a little further. His proposal was that a successful dropkick field goal scrimmaged from beyond the 30 yard line, should be worth four points. Murray Kasic thought the dropkick idea was brilliant and that it would add a new dimension to the kicking game while creating new scoring opportunities. Unfortunately, Murray did not have a vote in the matter. Henry, it appeared, would need to create his own league if he were to implement his own rules.

When Duncan Chambers talked with Henry he did his best to let him down gently. On the whole Henry took his rejection quite well but still believed that some of the geometric rules were inconsistent. Duncan asked, "what rule is inconsistent?"

"Crossing the plane," Henry excitedly yelped.

"What are you talking about?" Duncan countered.

"You have the sidelines, right? And you have the goal line too. If the ball crosses the plane of the opponents goal line on an offensive possession, it's called a touchdown. In other words, the scoring team is considered to be in the end zone, by virtue of the ball crossing the plane. And this is regardless of whether the player is actually in the end zone. But on the sidelines, it's the complete opposite, right? If a player catches a pass with the ball way, way over the plane of the sideline, but he keeps both feet in the field of play, the player is considered to be in the field of play. Not out of bounds."

Duncan said, "yeah, but Henry."

"And even if that player who caught that pass falls out of bounds, after having possession and maintains possession, he's still considered to be in the field of play. It's insane."

"But you can't take away sideline athleticism on catches, that's a huge part of the game," Duncan said.

"Of course. What I'm getting at is the idea of the plane at the goal line. It's wrong. That's why it's called a touchdown, Duncan. You're supposed to physically get into the end zone and touch the ball down on the ground. They're not touchdowns anymore. They're most often, just scores," Henry railed.

"Sure, but that's 'cause the league has evolved, Henry."

"Exactly. That's what I'm trying to do, evolve the league."

That's the way it went for a good half an hour. Duncan was exhausted by the time Henry left. Henry was energized. He was just creating diversions. The magician had them all looking at the wrong hand.

Charlene was in the habit of rarely seeing Henry during the work week. But before all this football stuff started she would usually see him on the weekends. It was three weekends down, and one to go that month, and she still hadn't seen him. The last weekend they spent together was in Jacksonville. They attended a home game as guests of Deborah and Murray, in their private box. Charlene was beginning to suspect that Henry was more interested in his work with the Jaguars than he was with his own practice. She was also beginning to feel that he didn't have much time for her anymore. She needn't have worried that anything had changed, because all was as it always was. Truth be told, Henry never did have any time for her, period. She was useful to him and that was all. But any emotion even approaching the feeling of love was just not possible for him.

Making love with her was becoming more and more difficult for Henry. He experienced no physical problems. It was just that Charlene's wholesome beauty and somewhat aquiline nose did nothing to stir him. Her nostrils were regular and ordinary and her ear lobes were pierced and relatively petite. Anyone else would have been very happy to look at her lovely face in the throes of passion. Not him. No, he wanted something else.

It would not be entirely accurate to say he fantasized with great lust and abandon. For him it was more of a plan than a fantasy, because anything he thought about was a future possibility. So when his mind conjured images of various nasal accoutrements, he truly intended to create them. Every kind of shocking apparatus fabricated to enlarge a nostril or lengthen an ear lobe was considered. Rubber nose washers, graduated in size, were designed in his head. These were to be used to slowly and painlessly cause disfigurement. He actually thought it would be very romantic to present a finely measured set of these nostril wideners to someone as a gift.

The really sad thing for this couple was that Charlene also harbored unspoken desires. Though she loved Henry, she was never excited by him. His scrawny appearance, coupled with his stark hairlessness was not what she really wanted. She wanted a real man, a man who could make her feel safe and protected. As far as she was concerned Henry had the body of a twelve year old boy. Twelve year old boys didn't turn her on. And they sure didn't make her feel safe.

In these unspoken matters, they were not very different from most couples. There was, time and again, at least one area of every relationship that was vague and unclear. Men and women offered much lip service to openness and honesty but the proof of the pudding was in the eating. One partner never told the other partner everything. The reason was one of vulnerability. Survival instincts never allowed for that. Divulging absolutely everything meant giving up control and entering a state of serfdom beholden to one's master.

These two, well educated in the ways of the psyche, were every bit as guilty as the average couple. They kept secrets. Behaviors were modified to placate the other. The problem was the behavior modification ran on a one-way street. The weaker partner made all the changes, while the stronger one felt entitled. When this happened, there was always conflict. First, within the mind and soul of the weaker partner anger would arise. The next thing to be affected would be the weaker partner's physical reality as the person was molded by the pressure. After that, resentment would creep into the mix. This would cause further conflict resulting in more resented behavior modification. Then the weaker person would begin to unwittingly express the helplessness in antisocial behavior. Alcoholism, drug addiction, infidelity and gambling were just a few of the problems that could occur.

Charlene was beginning to express her helplessness by first fantasizing and then acting out her dreams of ecstatic, serene, secretive sex. She discovered that the secrecy and sex she craved were more addictive than she anticipated. The sex was satisfying but the secrecy was electrifying. To be able to descend into the muck and hump like a warthog, in complete anonymity, was the feast her soul desired. Only many years later would she realize that the meal was empty calories. If she had given up her relationship with Henry, she would have cured herself. Eventually, the lack of nutrition in all those meals would have steered her to a more wholesome and balanced diet. In the meantime, she would have her just desserts.

Though rich enough, she enjoyed the everyday spartan surroundings of Motel 6. She wasn't making love. She was having sex. Making love was reserved for expensive hotels, she reasoned. Rutting like a pig always felt better when someone left the light on for you.

Simon Leathem was a very likable guy. Even Henry liked him. He was a large, powerful, muscular man, who was also thoughtful, intelligent and spiritually philosophical. Born a Presbyterian in Utah, the divergence of the external and domestic religious influences made him a searching skeptic.

In high school, Simon played both ways for the football team. He was better than all his opponents and easily the best offensive lineman in the state. He could play any offensive line position but always preferred to play center, which seemed to mirror his basic diplomatic personality. He never veered too far to the left or the right politically. He always sought common ground in any kind of dispute. This measured and passive nature of his nearly crushed him on a number of occasions. But in the meantime, he thrived.

A scholarship to a Southern Baptist University in Virginia followed his stellar high school career. He majored in religion and philosophy, hoping to find his path to destiny in the service of others. Slowly but surely, his skepticism gave way to a new and interrogating faith. Many of his fellow Jaguar players were believers too. That made for a lot of prayer meetings between team meetings and practices and games.

Prayer meetings were something of interest to Henry, and he was delighted when Simon came to see him for tweaking. He, as a shrink, wanted to get to the bottom of this apparent dichotomy between caring Christian selflessness and beating the shit out of opponents on the football field. So, his ongoing consultations with Simon were a breath of fresh air compared with the usual complaints and problems he heard. The center and fourth-down snapper also had lingering issues he needed to settle.

Henry elicited from Simon most of the facts concerning his homosexual affairs. He was clearly bisexual, having had only heterosexual experiences in his late teens. But later, in his twenties, he succumbed to homosexual fantasies and acted them out intermittently. He was troubled by his double life. He wanted children and he definitely wanted to have a stable heterosexual marriage. However, he couldn't envisage giving up his latent proclivities. When probed more deeply he admitted that he truly didn't want to give them up, and it was the not wanting to give them up which was really bothering him.

As his story unfolded in fifty minute segments, Henry considered how fickle and confusing life was. Here was this behemoth before him, six foot five, 295 pounds, strong as an ox, yet as timid as a lamb. Frightened of his own sexuality, he came to him for help. Henry wondered why he needed help at all. Had it been Henry's situation he wouldn't have viewed it as a problem. He would go ahead and get the girl. Get the family. And get off however and whenever he wished.

Simon spoke of only a couple of experiences with another boy when he was about twelve or thirteen. But these were only masturbation sessions, he said. While these sessions occurred, they were both viewing pornographic pictures of women, and there was no contact between them. Henry wasn't sure if Simon was telling the truth. But after a few conversations in which he made it impossible for him to lie without detection, he was satisfied that this man mountain was completely honest.

"So, you pulled your puddin' with another boy when you were twelve." That was probably not the most tactful thing Henry ever said. But that was how he operated.

Pinpointing the exact time or the specific incident that might have altered his sexual orientation was a waste of time to Henry. He was a nostril freak himself and he didn't care where the fixation came from. He liked it. He was not about to relinquish his pleasure for a psychological breakthrough. This monster Adonis though, he was different, and Henry had to keep him positively focused. At least until the season was over. Henry wanted to know what was happening in his life at that point. Was he involved with women or men at that moment? Was he having relations with both sexes? What were his fantasies?

He explained that since training camp started he had not been with a man, but he recently began a torrid affair with a woman which he found very exciting. He was concerned about his emotions and feelings, and his fantasies too. "Emotionally, it's women all the way, but it's funny Doc, when I'm having sex with this woman, I'm thinking about penises. Is that normal?"

"It is for you, which makes it completely normal and acceptable," Henry answered.

"Another thing. I have no romantic feelings for men, no emotional attachment whatsoever. I mean, I'd never take a guy out for dinner, not that way anyway. But when I'm having sex with a guy I never fantasize about women at all. Why is that?"

"I guess because when you're with a man you're acting out your penis fantasy," Henry said.

"And when I'm with a woman?"

"You wish you were with a man," Henry stated.

"So, I'm more gay than straight?"

"No. How can I best express this? Sexually, you prefer the bat to the glove, but emotionally, you'd rather have a burrito than a banana. I want you to consider what I'm about to say very seriously, 'cause I'm not joking. Think about this now. Do you think you'd be satisfied in every possible way if you married and had a family with a beautiful woman? A beautiful woman who had that one extra thing you love? A big boner?"

Simon wondered about Henry. He wondered how this little man could be so disgusting and crass and yet so accurate, as he answered, "A dream come true."

Henry went on to explain that in the absence of finding and falling in love with the perfect hermaphrodite, who could also conceive, he would need to come to terms with his sexuality. He told him that if he wanted to pilot the flight of his life, he needed to accept that both the fuselage and the hangar would figure prominently in it.

Then the conversation turned in its usual direction, toward philosophy and religion. As usual, when the conversation turned there was precious little time left for them to talk. And football was one topic they hadn't yet broached, because Simon's on-field performance was exemplary.

CHAPTER 10

Jon Buchanan was a methodical and meticulous fact checker. He was slightly obsessive about it but that just made him a better reporter. This feeling he had stuck in his craw about Henry Collier just forced him to do more of the same. Virtually no article ever written about Dianne Black or Cameron Timchuk escaped his scrutiny. He read everything he could find but kept returning to his gnawing, yet vague sense that something wasn't right about the relationships Henry had with the two athletes.

Sitting in front of his computer, coffee and Oreos at his side, he delved once again, and he promised himself for the very last time, into the cyberspace of information about the two Canadians. This was it. He was not about to waste any more time on a hunch which wasn't panning out. Admittedly he'd been wrong before, but not too often. And this looked to be shaping up to be one of those disappointing dead ends when the phone rang.

It was Henry. He called from his car to express his regret that he must have appeared to be avoiding an interview. Duncan Chambers had given him his phone number but he'd been too busy to call until then. He told Jon he'd be pleased to grant him an interview. "I'll be in Jacksonville tomorrow. Can we do something tomorrow?"

"Sure," Jon sensed something inherently disingenuous in Henry as he said, "good timing." I'm doing my homework on you now." There was an almost imperceptible hesitation on the other end of the line, Jon thought.

"Great. I should be available at four o'clock. Is that okay?" Henry asked.

"Sure, whereabouts?"

"The GLADES. You know it?"

"Yeah, I know where it is. See you at four." What a timely phone call that was. Jon's energy was flagging prior to speaking to Henry, and he was just about to give up. But now he felt like he just downed a dozen Red Bulls.

Synchronicity was much more than a concept to Jon. He wholeheartedly believed in it. He always said things don't just happen randomly. They happen for a specific reason. To him, synchronicity was real and present time karma but not the distant karma of another lifetime. He believed people were always creating their immediate futures, which congealed into synchronicity and their reactions to that synchronicity would shape their distant karma. Henry's phone call at that very moment was one of those synchronistic events. Even the means of transmission was symbolic to Jon. Henry used a cellular phone to confirm an intuitive and cellular certainty within him.

He still had one Oreo and a quarter cup of coffee left when he finally spotted it. He berated himself for not spotting it sooner. As he scanned through the information on the websites he noticed that in three different newspaper articles and two unrelated websites, all supposedly written by different people, there was one phrase or variation of that phrase in common.

In a fan-based website created for Dianne Black, Jon spotted the phrase 'dedication rarely seen' which was eerily close to 'rarely seen dedication' that stood out on the Cameron Timchuk site. Two of the newspaper articles also had one common piece of phraseology. One called Dianne 'deafeningly dedicated' because she was always tuned in to her music. The other article mentioned Cameron's 'unheard of dedication'. Was Jon just clutching at straws? He didn't think so. It would have been quite a coincidence, Jon thought, for four different people in different parts of the country, at different times, to land upon almost the very same type of phrase. He knew enough about writing styles and pitfalls to recognize and be quite convinced that the same person wrote them all. And now he was pretty sure he knew who that person was. Tomorrow's interview couldn't come fast enough for Jon.

Driving home, Henry considered his options and all the possible scenarios that might unfold. How much did this reporter know? Maybe he was trying to be cute or just plain courteous when he talked about doing his homework. Besides, what could he possibly have discovered? Henry had been very careful with the fabrications he posted. Technically, everything was up to par. Dianne Black was dead, and Cameron Timchuk was a vagrant who seemed to have disappeared off the ends of the earth.

"Enough of this nonsense!" he said aloud, as he quickly regained his equilibrium and fell back into his normal unemotional state. Loving his new life with the athletic elite, he could ill afford to have any problems develop now. The trust he engendered with the players overflowed into their personal lives, as he knew it would. A round of golf here, a barbecue there, and in no time at all he was attending the wild parties he envisioned

The Skater

from the very beginning. Blow, booze, babes and weed were what Henry was growing accustomed to in his new life.

He cultivated his sense of personal power by being a part of it all, yet remaining on the periphery. His quirky personality kept him comfortably on the sidelines, while appearing to be on the field with the others. Full disclosure was a blasphemy to him. He never, ever disclosed himself to anyone under any circumstances. He disseminated self truths like he fed goldfish. A tiny sprinkle on the surface to be devoured before any meaningful depth could be reached.

Being a psychologist afforded him an implicit line of defense not enjoyed by the average layperson. It never ceased to amaze him that people assumed he was psychologically pure by virtue only of his professional status. They were foolish to think that and he was ill behooved to correct them. People existed for his pleasure and his whim. The Queen herself could not possibly have felt any more entitled. His smugness flowered as his murky motives grew deeper roots in his soul.

He had grand plans for these athletic men who played games for a living. He would show them games. They had no idea what game they were playing. Such was his omnipotence. He knew well what they thought of him and he understood the fickleness of their recent good fortune. When losing once again became a more constant companion they would turn on him. But it would be too late. He would have already had his way with them, and he would be gone, happy to have made their acquaintance, broken their spirit and grown his portfolio.

He really had stepped into the big league. In the past, he engineered a number of unlawful enterprises from various telephone scams to slick pyramid schemes. But this was different, both in its scope and its potential reward. When this seed germinated he would no longer be able to hide the harvest.

He thought about what he would do when he was filthy rich. He knew he would still need to work with people, because that was his raison d'etre. Like the alcoholic who cannot imagine living without the bottle, Henry could not see himself living without a battle. He was the quintessential cerebral gunslinger. He was quicker on the draw, and he had a bigger gun. This was as close as he ever got to placing any importance at all in the Big Bang theory.

Four players were being softened up by the middle of the season. Controlling people's actions by reprogramming them was no problem for him. These football types were easy pickings, mainly because they had more money than they deserved and they were still greedy for more. They told Henry they had a right to as much money as the market would bear.

He agreed wholeheartedly with them, and he would be exercising his right to theirs in due course.

Ponzi schemes were brilliant because they were so simple. As long as the perpetrator gained the absolute trust of the victims, their fate was sealed. It was said once, by G.B. Shaw, that when you rob Peter to pay Paul, you can always count on the support of Paul. The support of Peter, of course, would be financed by robbing Fred and on and on and on. Henry had already 'invested' forty thousand dollars from his Four Horsemen. They willingly gave him $10,000 each, on a written guarantee that within six months they would see a 15 to 20% return on their investment. Ten thousand dollars to these overpaid athletes was like a hundred bucks to a regular working guy. No wonder they were parted with their money so easily. Six months down the road they would each be the recipient of a $2000 unregistered and non-taxable dividend. Henry planned to continue to pay out his 'dividends' until he really had them hooked. At that point, he reasoned, they would almost part with their family jewels to collect more coin.

He reckoned it would take him two seasons to see his plan through to fruition. By that time, he considered he would likely have another two or three investors in the plan. He was going to need a lot of money to finance his new life in the Cayman Islands. He had already established residency there a couple of years ago. With enough money, anyone could get in. It was a snap. He already owned a home on Grand Cayman. Once there, he planned to procure weekend retreats on Little Cayman, and Cayman Brac. Cuba wasn't too far away either, and money had a Spanish accent in Castro's fiefdom. And the women he could buy, had bought, were intoxicating to him. The wide, flaring nostrils; the tawny Latin lobes; the memories fueled his ardor. He prognosticated about what the future held for him. He had assumed the persona. He was 'Nostrildamus'.

Simon Leathem's outreach program to help substance abusers was in its third year of operation. He ministered to many people and genuinely believed. He saved a lot of souls from certain torment, and sometimes death. He was born to help his fellow men and women. It was in the very fabric of his being to be of service to others.

It was at the hospital in Shreveport that he and Charlene first crossed paths. She was the dedicated psychiatrist, and he the sympathetic and caring minister. In fact, Charlene was the woman he told Henry about in their last discussion. It was a good thing too that he hadn't divulged any details, like how or where they met. Because surely Henry would have twigged to the identity of his lover. That would have made the weekend Simon planned somewhat distasteful, in light of Henry's generosity in handing him the key to his house and the remote control for his garage.

The Skater

Henry was spending the weekend in Florida anyway, and his house wasn't that far from Shreveport. It seemed like a good idea to Simon. So he accepted Henry's offer. The only thing Henry knew was that Simon was going out of town to minister to his forlorn flock and be of service to others. That he was also going to service Charlene, he did not know.

Charlene would have found herself emotionally torn, had she known to whose home her current insertion person was taking her. She had not, to that point, even crossed the threshold of Henry's house, as he was always the one to make the drive up from Baton Rouge. She wanted to see it and asked many times to see it but circumstances always seemed to mitigate against it. Of course, Henry didn't want her anywhere near his home, and least of all inside it. She was completely unaware that Henry held a total aversion to sharing his space with anyone, including her.

Simon arrived to pick her up just as she was closing her office. He waited out in the parking lot with the engine running and the air on. They settled for a short, moist kiss as Charlene sat down beside him. He suggested they get something to eat before they begin their trip south. She wasn't hungry, so a compromise was reached to drive for an hour and then stop somewhere to grab a bite. Though they agreed to wait an hour before stopping, Simon would definitely have preferred to eat right away and he had a few good reasons.

The first reason was that he was ravenous right then, not an hour out. The second and third reasons, he felt, would directly affect his sexual performance, which he knew would commence as soon as the two of them were inside Henry's place. He didn't like to have sex on a full stomach because, for some reason, his penile sensation was anything but sensational. He reckoned that it probably had something to do with his digestion and temporary bloating. He most enjoyed his pelvic thrusting on an empty stomach, after a voluminous bowel movement.

The perplexing thing to him was that he did not have the same concerns when engaged in man sex. He ruminated on everything Henry had explained to him. He decided that again it was the emotional aspect of his sexuality which caused most of his issues. The very idea of losing control and breaking wind in the presence of a female sex partner was abhorrent to him. Farting with a naked male didn't seem to bother him as much, so long as the wind broken was not an ill wind.

As the Lincoln Navigator rolled down the highway toward Baton Rouge they both spoke excitedly about their respective weeks. He noticed that a little bit of the edge was somehow missing from Charlene's demeanor. He didn't mention it. New lovers seldom broached potentially unsettling talk. That would have taken the edge off their lust making for sure. With his left hand on the steering wheel, and his right hand in her wheelhouse, he soon forgot about her vague sullenness.

Charlene was a little unsettled as she pondered the end of her relationship with Henry. She wasn't sure if this particular tryst would pan out, but she was certain of one thing. For all of Henry's attributes, he was not capable of giving himself to her completely. She always felt he was not entirely turned on by her. This imposing looker she was with now, though, definitely was. She sensed his delight in her, her body and her soul. She was, obviously, senseless. As she furtively glanced into the drivers seat at his largely outlined and thinly veiled skin cylinder, she seeped through his fingers, unaware of his troubling penile preoccupation.

Simon didn't get to put on the feed bag for about ninety minutes, but he didn't mind at all. A steaming vixen at his side, a tumultuous erection in his pants and a mental picture of his perfect woman, aided and abetted his gastronomical ambivalence. Maybe if he didn't eat too much, he thought, then with a glass or two of wine, he might be able to circumvent the dreaded bloat.

Charlene had never enjoyed a car trip so much. Anytime she traveled with Henry, the subjects were always the same; him, shop talk, psychobabble, and him again. What she was enjoying was that she and Simon were actually talking out loud about what they were doing. It was almost like play-by-play commentary of their manual ministrations upon each other. She was having the time of her life and the empirical evidence of it was pooling on the upholstery.

If ever there was a time to use the cruise control, this was the time. He slowed the car to sixty-nine in a Freudian attempt at simultaneously navigating and fornicating. With the cruise on he was now free to shift his right leg wide to rub Charlene's slim, ivory shin with his golden muscled calf. For a few moments, he suspended his homosexual fantasy to bask in the aromatic reality of what she was doing.

Charlene was fast approaching a level of intoxication she had never before reached. She was compelled to remove the damp cotton bikini as a prelude to spreading her lithesome legs east and west, as they traveled south. Her right hand busily began her favorite concerto, which never failed to climax on the very highest octave, while her left hand sought out and conducted the maestro himself. She gawked and she gasped at the sight of the man and the music, certain she could handle her messiah.

With his hand now free, he was able to release her heavy and pendulous breast from its lilac captor. He held it timidly in his large palm, entranced with its texture and density. Her taupe and tightening aereola, wide and sunken, raised a pink and pencil eraser like nipple. He could ill afford an attempt to kiss it while driving, so he settled for gently bending

The Skater

it, amazed at its flexibility. He was awestruck with her fragrance, and the depth and breadth of her luxurious savanna. Her painted nails vanished into the rainforest as her saluting left palm found but could not leave its post. The syrup season had arrived as the sap ran freely through the maple she had left uncut. And the forest floor was awash as the monsoon had finally come.

Later, unbeknownst to her, she buoyed atop the bluish hues of Henry's private lap pool. She and her lover, immersed in the calming amniotic sea, her breasts afloat. She smiled the smile of a woman come home. Her epiphany occurred as her wake slowly swam away from her. She loved him and though she didn't know it yet, he loved her too.

The scene was ecstasy and serenity, but it was not secrecy. Only a fool, and surely Simon was, would believe that Henry would give away anything without getting more back in return. The cameras rolled throughout the weekend.

CHAPTER 11

Jon was a half hour early arriving at the restaurant. He always enjoyed making himself comfortable and getting halfway through his beer before the interviewee arrived. It gave him time to recheck his notes, verify the facts and outline the course of his questioning. In this case, he still wanted to write a fitting piece on Henry's contribution to the recent success of the Jaguars, but also and perhaps more important to him, he was looking to ferret out the weasel. If he concluded that he was 100% sure about Henry then he would begin an all-out quest to find Cameron Timchuk. And once that interview was in the bag, Henry would be too.

He could see it now, in his mind's eye. Perhaps a Sports Illustrated feature awaited him. Honors, of course, would follow as his exposé had uncovered a cancer within the system and a malicious, disingenuous manipulator had been exposed. A barnacle on the side of society was what Jon thought of Henry. He gave himself another minute or two to fantasize and then he brought his mind back to the work at hand. He expected to meet a formidable foe but wasn't sure how that foe would present himself. He'd heard that Henry was really sharp, and he knew that he needed to be sharper, because he'd no doubt get only one shot at him.

There was nothing quite like the thrill and the anticipation he felt whenever he was trying to exact the truth from someone who was determined not to share it. It must have been all those crime shows he used to watch that made this part of his job so attractive and exciting. Truth was the most important concept in Jon's life, and he couldn't recall a time when it wasn't. He well understood subjective reality. Everyone had their own spin, no matter who was doing the spinning or what was being spun. But truth as a philosophical concept was something completely different.

Truth was enormous and all encompassing, because it shaped the physical reality that people lived. It didn't matter to Jon what truth someone believed. True laws applied to everyone equally, whether they were accepted and believed or not. The law of motion applied even to those who chose not to believe it. Gravity affected astronauts and moon landing deniers equally. A flat earther would still circumnavigate the globe if he couldn't get off the ship. The ignorant savage who didn't believe and couldn't conceive of radio waves still had them passing through his body. At some point in everyone's life, the truth of the motivation of one's soul would have to be declared. Jon believed that but Henry did not.

What a contrast the two made when they met. John stood six foot one and weighed two hundred pounds. Henry was five foot five and seventy eight pounds lighter. Jon's curly black hair was fashionably short, while Henry's was a little too long and unfashionably unkempt. The color of Jon's skin was a healthy cappuccino and Henry's looked like spattered spilt milk. As they seated themselves after shaking hands, Henry was cool and unmoved. Jon was momentarily overcome with nausea, but gathered himself, still feeling the ache in his stomach. This was a true watershed moment for them both. Down through the centuries and all the world over, people from the past to the future would accept the mantle and enter the battle. What was the nature of this confrontation? It pitted a proverb against a lie, a prayer against a blasphemy, a blessing against a curse. This was a good man squaring off against a bad man.

Jon, since he was little, was very sensitive to the vibrations people emanated. Good intentions gave him warm and fuzzy goosebumps, from head to toe. Bad intentions always left him nauseated and weak. There was no doubt in Jon's mind, no doubt at all. He was looking directly into an empty vessel. This man had no soul, and was probably born without one, Jon thought. He was sure Henry was not cognizant that he was bereft of humanity. That, unfortunately, didn't make him any more lovable.

Henry knew who Jon was and every 'John' like him for that matter. He'd been dispatching these delusional losers all his life. Here was another adversary of questionable quality. He didn't know the exact nature of the 'goods' Jon had on him. So he would tread carefully and communicate stealthily to find out what it was.

Jon had come to believe, from his personal experience that people, by and large, look like what they really are. Their motives, the direction of their souls and the primary purpose of their lives shone through their faces. Someone who looked miserable usually was. And while a jovial person might indeed harbor fear or hide deep depression, the thrust of their lives was usually good and honest and it showed.

Henry was a tough read, as far as Jon was concerned. Yes, he looked like a weasel, but it seemed to be worse when he smiled, not when he frowned. He reasoned that it was because his frowns were not as phony as his smiles. Being aware of this, he listened very closely when he frowned and

The Skater

even closer when he smiled. His soft filmy teeth were probably the result of all the acidic lies that had crossed them. On a visceral level, alone, Jon fought a persistent squeamishness. Intellectually, he understood Henry to be quite bright, but he was certain that he was emotionally stunted, if not deranged or damaged in some way. As the interview progressed, he satisfied himself that he was beginning to take the measure of the man.

Jon appeared to Henry to be one of those real cool dudes who always got the girl. He was right. He could see Jon was tall and athletic looking, with a very straight, almost military look to him. He surmised that he was religious, because he wore a gold cross on a chain around his neck. He was single because he didn't leer at the gorgeous waitress like a married fool. He was temperate, one beer would suffice throughout the meal, and he would probably have two cups of coffee afterward.

"So, what brought you to the deep south from the great White North?" Jon asked of Henry as he studied him carefully.

"I like warm weather."

"You can get that in California."

"I can't write my own prescriptions in California," Henry told him.

"Even though you're not an M.D.? How does that work?" Jon was piqued.

"Louisiana and New Mexico, I think, also allows for writing scripts."

"Do you prescribe a lot of medication for your patients?" Jon didn't see the relevance or the importance of this.

"Not really, only when necessary."

"Any of the Jaguars depressed?" Jon twigged to the relevance now. It was a power thing.

"Not this season," Henry quipped. He was already tiring of Jon's transparency. "I keep them positive and focused and believing in themselves. It's really that simple."

"Well, the players seem pretty happy with you. I've spoken to a few of them. Nothing but good things to say." Jon couldn't completely conceal his disdain and revulsion, though he tried. He was sure Henry noticed and he really didn't care. He wasn't trying to win a friend. "How is it different for you, as far as your approach and methodology is concerned, when you're dealing with athletes in a team sport, as opposed to individual athletics?"

"There is no difference whatsoever except the football guys are bigger and meaner," Henry tried to joke.

"But wouldn't that, in and of itself, change how you talk to them? Some of those guys are pretty intimidating. I know. I have to try to get information from them."

"So, you handle them differently from, say, a female gymnast, for example?" Henry asked.

"Absolutely."

"Then there must be something you're afraid of. Correct?"

"Of course. I'm afraid of not getting a story. It's my job. I'm a reporter."

"So you need to sort of adjust your tactics depending on who it is, right?" Henry was asking the questions now.

"That's the most effective way," Jon answered, realizing that Henry was turning and leading the conversation.

"So, how are you deceiving me right now to get the story you want?" Henry asked. Jon had one thought only in his mind at that moment. And it was that this little dirt stick was one tricky little prick. He told himself to give his head a shake and sharpen up. "I'm pretending to like you," Jon said.

"Everybody does that. I mean, what are you hiding and what are you trying to expose?" Henry was still asking the questions.

"I'm not hiding anything. And I'm not trying to expose anything. All I want to know is how football players differ from skiers and skaters. Or, at least, how you handle them differently."

"I told you. No difference," Henry spouted, knowing for certain now that this Buchanan knew something about Black and Timchuk. What he knew was entirely and only what Henry wanted him to know. So, he surmised Jon had done his homework. So what? Henry was the teacher, and Jon the student. All the information Jon had access to had been carefully crafted and deftly planted. "I'll bet if you talked to Dianne Black or Cameron Timchuk they'd tell you exactly what Skeet Leach said. They'd confirm what I'm telling you." Henry called his bluff. He wanted it out in the open. He wanted Jon to admit that with one dead, and the other disappeared, it didn't matter what he thought he knew.

"Dianne Black is dead," Jon said.

"Oh, that's too bad," Henry said. "I guess you'll never get to verify what I'm saying."

"Well, Timchuk's not dead," Jon was baiting him now.

"Shame about him. Lots of problems, depressed, and alcoholic. Nobody knows where he is, apparently," Henry concluded.

"Well, I'm gonna have a little look for him this weekend. Matter of fact, I'm flying to Toronto later tonight. So maybe I can finally immortalize you in print." More than seeing a flicker in Henry's eyes, Jon just felt it.

"Good luck. Ever been to Toronto?"

"Quite a few times, actually," Jon said, as Henry was clearly caught off guard. This big super sleuth was going to find a derelict? In a city he probably didn't know very well? Henry didn't think so, as he volunteered, "let me know on Monday how you make out."

"Don't worry, I will," Jon said, and proceeded to finish his meal and order his second coffee.

Henry wondered whether Jon was actually going to Toronto. Maybe he was just trying to shake him up a bit. Three hours later, he stopped wondering as he watched Jon exit a cab, carry-on over his shoulder. He headed straight for the WestJet counter. Henry wasn't worried. Henry never worried.

When he arrived home as the weekend was winding down, Henry wondered how much extra his cleaning woman would have to do. A cursory look around the house told him she wouldn't have to do very much more than the usual. At least Simon had the courtesy to strip the bed and throw the dirty linen in the hamper. There were a few dishes in the sink but nothing major for Joanna to worry about.

Henry liked Joanna, his barely legal cleaning woman. He helped her get her green card, and she was extremely grateful. She was so grateful that sometimes she spent an hour or more polishing the walnut dining table, so the four fleece cloths would slide easily under her hands and knees for him. She always received an extra bonus in her paycheck when Henry helped her polish. Back when she was hired, he told her that there were two others who also worked for him. There was a pool boy and a gardener. She understood the full extent of what her domestic duties would be when Henry told her that he desperately wanted to place her on his staff. She told him she would enjoy this new position.

He wondered if Simon saw the pool boy during the weekend. When he gave him the key he considered calling his pool boy to cancel his regular Saturday visit, but decided against it. A little temptation was good for the soul, they said. If his plan bore any fruit, Simon's next visit to the shrink would be an interesting one indeed. After all, he did say that he was attracted to men and women. So, would he be willing to engage both of them at once? Henry would know soon enough.

Video surveillance was a godsend for him. Not only did it increase his security, it also decreased his property insurance. But the added bonus of spying on people gave him an exquisite rush. Along with all his other psychological propensities, voyeurism was another to be added to the list. It wasn't just the watching alone that excited him. It was doing it in complete secrecy. The victim's awareness would have spoiled everything, because it would have exposed him.

Why was it that people, who would never undress in front of others, would undress with no compunction whatsoever in front of a dog or a cat? He thought the reason was that an animal's consciousness was lower than a person's. They didn't have the awareness to challenge a human's sense of decency. People would lie, cheat and steal in front of Rover, because there was no consciousness to challenge or shame their own.

He used the weekend getaway ploy before, with some of the other players and they proved to be quite entertaining to him. There was always the possibility of using the recordings as leverage at a later date. And, of course, he never missed an opportunity.

Henry never had to worry about lying, cheating or stealing because his ego, which had constructed a false conscience, was incapable of shame. If he had ever been videotaped doing something private or untoward, he might have reacted in anger, as others surely would have done. The difference was that his anger would have been manufactured from his supercilious nature and not from any sense of propriety. The average person might have wished to get even. Getting even was never in Henry's playbook, because his purpose was to get the advantage in all situations. His ego would never have allowed otherwise. Getting even implied beginning the exercise from a position of weakness before becoming an equal. Whenever he found himself in a situation in which he was not superior, in his own mind, it was only because he hadn't bothered to wield his own supremacy in the first place.

Shame could never enter into his experience of reality. Shame and the embarrassment it engendered, grew from an acknowledgment of wrongdoing, and that was anathema to him. The choice between right and wrong was a very easy one for him to make. Whichever choice provided the most enjoyment was always the one he made. When all the earth and all its riches existed only for his pleasure, then any choice was valid, no matter the consequences.

Guilt was another state of mind foreign to him. He couldn't accept blame for any act he committed because he existed outside the concept of fault. Consequences were just results, and any result simply occurred due to a cause. If he caused an unfortunate result, that was all that transpired. Feeling guilty about one's actions was just human frailty, to him.

Upon discovery, as in the case of Alan Bean, who left his last thought about Egyptian archaeology on the crown molding, he always managed to escape retribution. It wasn't surprising, since most of those who were injured by him were inherently weak. Further psychological battering at his hands only served to make them more helpless. Professional athletes were helpless too, but much more likely to be volatile and wreak havoc in their wake. He pondered these things, but as usual came to the conclusion that there was nothing he couldn't handle. During his sessions with the players he soon found out that each 'inner child' was really a 'spoiled brat' and their tantrums could be used against them quite effectively.

How could he not have been confident? He was already in possession of their money, and they thanked him ever so much for the opportunity. He got the whole idea of a mining exploration scam from talking with

The Skater

Charlene's father, Gerry Kempf Junior. At the time her father was involved in a new venture and was recruiting investors. Gerry Kempf never did manage to convince Henry to invest. He didn't want to have too many ties to Charlene, and besides, he preferred to keep his money in 'unregistered' plans.

Jon's flight arrived at Pearson international Airport just after ten o'clock on Friday evening. It was unseasonably warm and for a moment he thought about what it would be like to live in Toronto. Then he remembered the winters. He preferred to stay warm and risk the occasional hurricane than freeze his ass off for the luxury of avoiding them.

He found it interesting, the rationalizations people made to explain their decisions. After all, snow brought with it lots of shoveling. Not to mention slick, icy roads that could just as easily kill you as a hurricane. Ice storms too brought down power lines and left folks cold and frozen in their own homes. It appeared to him that people could get used to just about anything they experienced. Once it was experienced, he felt, it became their reality and psychic inertia took over.

He came to believe, through his years of spiritual expansion, that things which appear random on this plane are anything but random on a higher one. He was born Jon Buchanan, but why? His soul and his essence, his spirit, the very properties that made him who he was, his higher power, why was it propelling his body and not someone else's? His conclusion was that a soul energizes a body knowing exactly what that person will encounter in life and what choices will have to be made.

So, here he was in Toronto on a mission to find a derelict. He was presented with a choice, and he easily could have let it slide. But he didn't. He made the decision to follow his instincts. That's who he was. As surely as Henry was driven to exploit people, he was driven to expose them.

But for what appeared to be random on this plane, he could have been born into any number of different situations. He could have been born white. He could have been brought into this world a woman, in another country, of another culture, speaking a different language and practicing a different religion. That was the reason he could never understand racism, sexism, bigotry and the like. He felt that, but for random chance on this plane, his soul could have experienced a totally different reality. These are the thoughts that preoccupied him as his cab made its way to his hotel.

He drank a couple of beers in his room while he relaxed, muted the TV and watched in silence. After ordering a corned beef on rye and a China black tea from room service, he hopped in the shower. He would need a good night's sleep, and he was sure to get it, once sedated with his holy triumvirate of beer, beef and ablutions.

By noon on Saturday Jon had visited the Salvation Army hostel and two other missions, with no luck whatsoever in finding anyone who'd even heard of Cameron Timchuk. Saturday had begun to look like a bust. He called, looking for an old friend at the Sun, only to be told that Serge was out in Vancouver and had been there for two years. Jon was hungry. He found himself in Chinatown. What could have been more synchronistic than that? He ate a great meal, a plate of Szechuan chicken and left a big tip. He caught a cab and headed for 52 division to see if maybe someone on the force might be able to help him. What a blessed stroke of luck that turned out to be.

The desk sergeant, Pierre Dupont, told him that two officers rounded up some people off the streets the night before. Some of them ended up in detox. They wouldn't be back on duty again until seven o'clock. Sgt. Dupont suggested Jon come back about 6:30 PM to see him. He would let him speak to the two cops then, he told him.

Jon went back to his hotel with the Sun, the Star and the Post. He read the sports sections first for obvious professional reasons. The Blue Jays were not in the playoffs, as usual. The Raptors season was about to begin, as usual, and the Maple Leafs were supposed to have a better season. As usual.

Setting the alarm for 4:30 PM, John took a nap. He felt satisfied with his day so far. Maybe he would be able to locate Timchuk after all. If he was in detox all night, he should be compos mentis enough to answer a few simple questions, Jon thought. That was really all he had gone to Toronto to do, ask a few simple questions. Questions like did he even know Henry. That was all he wanted and then he could put this all to bed.

He knew, though, deep in his bones that he was onto something big, that Henry was a liar and he was going to prove it. The Jaguars might suffer because of the scandal, but that wouldn't be his problem. He was just doing his job. And if he was completely wrong about Henry then he had only wasted his own time and money. But he would have done so being a good reporter. If he hadn't made the trip he would never know for sure. And he wouldn't have been able to live with that. The team ownership already had it in for him. Getting access would be even harder, he thought, but this whole shrink thing was an enormous story and might open new doors for him. Maybe even a book deal, a tell all about how he uncovered the truth and either saved or sank a pro franchise.

He drifted off to dreamland in ten minutes, or thereabouts. His last girlfriend, tennis shoes and a major-league umpire all made symbolic guest appearances in his mid-afternoon dream. The tennis shoes lay on first base. His girlfriend was up to bat. She wore an olive green V-neck fisherman's knit sweater. The umpire was jumping about screaming "infield fly rule."

The Skater

Not surprisingly, Jon watched it all unfold from his position, out in left field. Waking to the easy listening classics, he shook his head as he usually did when a dream was vivid in his mind. He didn't have time to analyze it and he always found that he could only get so far in his analysis anyway. The symbols he could figure out, but the whole meaning seemed to escape him almost every time. He chuckled to himself as the thought occurred to him that Henry Collier probably could analyze it for him. No matter. Henry would have his own nightmare to unravel pretty soon, if he had anything to do with it.

Why would a guy, a professional psychologist, risk everything, Jon contemplated. He had a thriving practice in Louisiana, yet he cooked the books, so to speak, in order to be on the staff of a professional football team. Why would he have done that? He played all this over in his mind many times since he answered the riddle the other night. "Go figure." That was the best he could do.

"Sgt. Dupont," Jon said.

"Yes, Mr. Buchanan. Nice to see you, and right on time." Sgt. Dupont explained to him that one of the officers he spoke of earlier in the day had called in sick, but the other officer, Pamela Yun, would be able to talk to him shortly.

When she introduced herself to Jon he was probably not too successful in hiding the fact that he was dumbstruck with her looks. She liked him too, but other than a courteous smile she gave no overt sign that she viewed him as anything other than an inquiring out-of-town reporter.

As Jon questioned her, he showed her a picture he printed from one of the websites. She told him she wasn't sure if that was the man, because Timmy, as she called him, was dirty and bearded. He was also a good few years older than the guy in the picture.

"His name is Cameron Timchuk. He used to be a figure skater. A few years back he was involved in a sex scandal. Had some knee operations," Jon said.

"Could be. The man had a noticeable limp," Officer Yun told him.

"Which leg did he favor?"

Pamela Yun was sizing up her interrogator. She liked him a lot. She liked the boiling passion just below the surface. "Left. Definitely the left. You think he's your guy?"

"It's sounding better all the time. Where can I find him?"

"He'll be in detox for a few days, at least. They won't let you see him while he's in there. How long are you here for?"

"Only till tomorrow night. Sure there isn't some way I can see him?" Jon was feeling a little bit deflated. He had to be back in Jacksonville for Monday morning.

"Sorry. They've got very strict rules, and they don't break them." She could almost see the wheels turning in his head, trying to figure out a way to solve his dilemma.

"No. I've got to be back by Monday," Jon said, dejectedly.

"Afraid I can't help you, Mr. Buchanan. Unless, you come back again," she said.

After a short silence, Jon answered. "Next weekend. I'll come back next weekend. I just need to ask him a couple of questions. Where can I find him when he's out?"

"Somewhere under the Gardiner," Yun offered.

"What?"

"He camps out sometimes, under the Gardiner Expressway. Different spots. Why don't I give you my number and you can call me when you come back. Pretty good chance I'll know where he is."

"That's great. Thanks." Jon was smiling again.

"You're more than welcome. Don't forget to call me."

"I won't. Talk to you next week."

Maybe fate was on Jon's side after all. For the price of a flight back the following week, he could confirm his suspicions and meet up with the sultry cop again. He didn't see a ring on her finger but guessed she wouldn't wear one on duty anyway. Things would turn out all right, he thought. Next weekend couldn't come fast enough.

Jon often pondered the possibility of fate. At this time in his life he contemplated some of the larger unknowns. What he came to believe was simply that fate presented the choices and the individual made the decisions. The karmic effects of the decisions made long ago, in another lifetime, created the big challenges in life. How those obstacles were dealt with was the domain of the soul, as it worked out the past and created Karma anew.

That policewoman had a profound impact on him. Not just sexually either. He felt something powerful in her presence. It was a kind of recognition. It was a kind of déjà vu. It was as if he knew her and was magnetically or spiritually drawn to her. Not drawn out of something new, but from something very old. He felt a certain peace when he spoke with her. She felt good. Not just her beauty, but the bounty beneath the surface. Had he met the one? He wondered.

Jon had no idea at all how he managed to sense the thoughts and feelings of others. It was a natural gift. This ability was a two edged sword. Sometimes it got him into situations not entirely good for him. Usually, that was a result of interpreting the feelings correctly, but misinterpreting the hidden intentions behind them. He projected his own emotionally charged thoughts into space, and thereupon was able to intuit the feelings and thoughts of others. As he thought back, he was sure his feelings about her were accurate. And even though she played the cool card, upon reflection, he could see she was as electrified as he was.

She could certainly pursue a career in law enforcement if she moved to the US, he thought. He might have to write for a smaller paper in a quieter community, or maybe his new syndicated column would afford him the luxury of a sedate, rural life. He was projecting way into the future and well beyond any reason to do so. But he couldn't help himself. He was awestruck. The power of his mind to manifest the ideas it contemplated was the stuff of myth and legend. To him, this was the true universal revelation. Nothing existed without thought. The unfolding of the visible, physical evidence would confirm the thoughts that had created it.

In his mind, in the blink of an eye, he experienced an entire lifetime with this woman. Love, children, mortgage, soccer practice, dance lessons, Disney World, college, grandchildren, and much, much more love he lived in that single moment. Had he met a terrible fate and been struck down dead at that very second, not even God could have taken away the life he had just lived.

Betrayal is something everyone encounters sooner or later. The most important aspect of its effect is how it is handled by the aggrieved. Gender certainly plays a role in the manner in which the pain is manifested. Men generally react much more violently than women. But that is not to say that some women aren't capable of causing grievous bodily harm or grievous emotional harm, for that matter. Some people, men and women both, take years, and even decades to sift through the sands of time long after the emotional dust has settled.

Henry's sense of betrayal was not normal, average or healthy. Actually, it was more like the feelings a school teacher might have after catching a student cheating. He didn't feel betrayed. He felt almost indifferently indignant that anyone would be brazen enough to challenge his authority. With no emotional bond between Charlene and himself, he felt only anger that she acted in her own self-interest. The interests of no one superseded his and he was a vengeful god. Betrayal usually brought emotional and sexual insecurity with it into the heart and mind. With him, this was not so. He reasoned that a god, such as he, could not be betrayed. They only betrayed themselves with cause and consequence. But it carried blame and fault with it, assigned by their god.

He poured himself a very tall whiskey with two ice cubes in his most favored burgundy goblet, as he sat down to watch 'Weekend at Henry's'. The surveillance camera at the front of his property recorded the big SUV as it turned into the driveway. Many minutes passed and nobody got out of the car. Finally, the driver side door opened and Simon stepped out. He closed the door and walked around the front of the vehicle, heading for the passenger side door. Henry could see the vague outline of a woman inside the car. She didn't move to open it on her own. She waited for Simon to do that, and Henry thought that she must be a real piece of work. A tremendous feeling of entitlement was the thought that went through his mind.

The large black door opened and out she stepped. Henry was stunned. He stared. He swallowed the big, dry, unbecoming swallow of a god become mortal. He gathered himself, simultaneously reaching for his drink and his immortality. As the rye warmed his belly and fuzzied up his head, he proceeded to monitor their coupling and uncoupling; their re-coupling and pube smacking; their skin licking and bedwetting. What bothered him more than anything was seeing their table polishing. For a moment he was transfixed. Simon was clearly a more forceful and adept polisher than he was. He imagined how Joanna would take to his wiping on and wiping off. This was as close as he ever came to pure, unbridled jealousy. If there had been a solitary spark of good within him, he probably would have stayed that way for a very long time. But there was none. And so he rebounded in complete denial of what had just flashed through him. The last vestige of light had gone out. The dusk had turned to darkness and his shadow had swallowed him up.

Sublimated anger could kill a person, but sublimated anger could kill other people too. His first inclination was to surgically manipulate, humiliate, and destroy the both of them. As usual, though, his first thought was not always his best. It almost made no difference to him what plan would be enacted to fix Charlene. She was easy prey. Simon would be a little more difficult to eradicate. Eradicate was the word he used for Simon and any other offending rodent, like Charlene.

He schemed to protract their emotional torture. Every turn of the screw was going to bring him immense delight. He thought about the exact moment when he would reveal their common knowledge of him. It was going to be Shakespearean in its pathos and irony. He was feeling much better, now that he had finished his second drink. He was, now, experiencing what he liked to refer to as 'rye syndrome'.

Under normal circumstances, he wasn't given to second-guessing himself. But on this day, he did. He walked the entire house, back and forth, assuring himself that there was indeed nothing present that could have made Charlene aware that it was in his house she had been humping. There was nothing. No letters, no bills, no ID, no photos, not even a phone book, which she could've used to look up Henry's address, since she was in Baton Rouge. In fact he never even used the speed dial on his phone. No phone numbers or names were displayed. He always made a call to a neutral number after any outgoing call. He did this so that the last call dialed could never be used against him. The recall was similarly circumvented by calling his home phone from his cell phone after any incoming call. There were no flies on him. But, if his intentions came to fruition, there would be plenty of flies on the two of them.

The secure compartment of his mind that handled Jon Buchanan and the Cam Timchuk business had not been unlocked since he followed him to the airport. Suddenly, the lock flew open and he examined the contents for possible outcomes. If Timchuk was found, what would he say? Was he even competent enough to speak with any kind of coherence? Was he dead? Was he missing? Those two thoughts gave him a conditional, but very satisfied feeling. He planned to call Buchanan in the morning and exude his usual anxious and irritating nonchalance. But after the shock of his earlier discovery he changed his mind. It was just minutes to midnight, and he thought that if he was slightly off his game himself, maybe he could disrupt the pretty boy reporter too.

What he was doing in those moments, after uncovering the sex secret, was struggling to regain his equilibrium. His normal state of equilibrium was not like that of others. His was not a balance of emotions, bobbing on the sea's surface, affected by winds and waves and the passing of ships in the night. His was a heavy, psychic pendulum swinging from indifference to wrath, through the plane of superiority. The pendulum was still swinging but its arc was altered toward the plane of frailty, and that he could not let stand.

He made the phone call. Jon didn't answer. The answering machine engaged, and Henry drummed his fingers, waiting for the message to start and finish so he could leave his own. He didn't leave the message as he had planned to do. Instead, he hung up in haste and exasperation.

Jon was lying on his bed as the phone rang. He smiled as he wondered who in the world it could be. He listened carefully as the message played, waiting for Henry's reply. It didn't come. He feigned disappointment to himself at the brushoff Henry had just given him. And after all the trouble he had gone to in tailoring his outgoing message especially for Henry. He listened to it play through once more, before he erased it.

"Henry, how are you? I just wanted to let you know I located your skater. Police are involved. I'll be speaking to him next week. Have a good night." Then he hit the button and went back to bed to dream about his own new and burgeoning involvement with the police.

CHAPTER 12

When Jeannie arrived at the office in the morning Henry had her reschedule all his afternoon appointments and all appointments for the rest of the week.
"What's happened?" she asked.
"I'm tired, Jeannie. I'm going to take the rest of the week off. Going to do some camping. Recharge. There won't be much for you to do here. So you're welcome to take the week off too. With pay, of course," Henry told her.
"Thanks Henry. I'll get started now. You've got Mrs. Delacroix scheduled for ten o'clock. Should I cancel her too?"
"If you can, that would be great. If not, I'll see her and leave afterward."
The first thing he did, once he was back in his office, was phone his mother. He got her voicemail, which she, like Jon, had updated. But her message was to all and sundry to refer any inquiries to her branch office. She said she would be away for two weeks. Henry was pleased. She must have taken that trip to Aruba, he thought. She talked about it when he spoke to her last month.

Edith had become somewhat of a phenom in the real estate market in the Niagara region, ever since she reverted to her maiden name and got her realtor's license. She was doing very well and was forever imploring him to come up for a visit. He was finally going to accept her invitation, whether she was there or not.

If ever there was a time when Henry Collier felt vulnerable, it was now after all the revelations of the last day. He tossed and turned most of the night, dreaming vividly incoherent dreams, interrupted sporadically by his growingly fearful thoughts. This was the first time he had ever really been under the gun. His realization that his past was small potatoes compared to this, both frightened and excited him. If he wanted to keep his reputation, his position with the Jaguars and his investment scam afloat he would need to step up to the plate and fix everything. And he needed to fix it right away.

Charlene and Simon were a work in process, and they could wait until the end of the week. They would have to wait until the end of the week, given the more pressing matter of the skater. He wished he could have asked Jon Buchanan where he found him but he knew that would only give him more reason to be suspicious. He would never have told him anyway. How the police were involved, he could only guess, but since the guy lived on the street it wasn't too far-fetched to think they might have played a role in locating him. He had to get to Timchuk before the reporter did. That was for certain. He would have to shut him up or buy him off or something, he thought.

He was released from St. Michaels Hospital on Monday afternoon. He didn't want to be there and they weren't able to keep him against his will. So Cameron Timchuk was back out on the street. He felt surprisingly clean and rejuvenated this time. The feeling of being clean and sober impressed him. He felt good for a change. He felt thirsty too. Change was exactly what he needed so he decided to beg for a little, to help keep him feeling good. In the blink of an eye, he went from feeling good to chasing a good feeling. His alcoholic mind was nearing the point of no return. The doctors told him he'd never last another year if he continued to drink. That made sense to him yesterday but less and less so with every passing minute.

If he could just get to that sweet spot again, it would be terrific. He'd hit it out of the park. His life would make sense and have meaning again. Meaning only existed in the sweet spot. Everywhere else was just swinging at air, swinging and missing. Striking out was the same as walking. Safe at home had even lost its allure. Home sweet home really wasn't. He didn't have a home anyway. So if he couldn't meet what life hurled at him in the sweet spot, there was no point in playing the game at all.

His flashes of lucidity were occurring less and less frequently. Some tiny detached segment of his mind told him it was the booze, but that wasn't the part that made him painless. So he didn't listen. In those moments, he knew there was so much that he had wanted to do with his life, and for his life, but it was what he had done to his life that caused the most pain. His efforts to pinpoint the exact times and the exact reasons for his plummet into the abyss were fruitless. It really didn't matter anyway. He was here, and the reasons were meaningless at that point.

What was important to him at that moment in time, was the same thing that was important at any other time he could now remember. Cocooned in oblivion was where he wanted to be. That was where he had to be. That was where the sweet spot was. He remembered some of his earlier days. Back then, the sweet spot was exquisite and new and exhilarating. What

The Skater

he was now dealing with was the very thing he was trying to deny. The sweet spot had soured long ago. That rare vintage he had cherished had long since turned to vinegar. Thinking he could get it back was the great delusion of all his ilk. Like all who had gone down before him, his liquid benefactor had prevailed. He preferred delusion to reality. At least delusion made him feel better. Unlike reality, dealing with delusion was effortless. The malt, the barley, the rye and the grape distilled his essence, and he couldn't escape.

He wouldn't live beyond a year if he didn't stop drinking, they said, but they gave him no guarantees of more time even if he stopped. Only one option would propel him into unknown territory and that was the difficult path of sobriety. He reasoned that it was better to die at his own hand than by the fickle finger of fate. Of course, his reasoning was flawed, because he never considered that it was his destiny to self-destruct.

His recurring blackouts had ceased to bother him a long time ago. They only seemed to bother him when he had something left to lose. Slowly but surely, he lost everything and with each loss he moved further and further away from sanity. Eventually, the only thing he had left to lose was his mind. His wet brain couldn't comprehend that his uncaring attitude toward his blackouts was proof that he no longer had a mind left to lose. Gone were the old days of wondering what he had said or done. The dread, the fear and the guilt had faded away as surely as the family, the friends and the good life. If that rare vintage had soured, then the blackouts became the new sugar he sought.

He was injured by others and that was a fact. But who amongst God's creatures could have possibly claimed otherwise? If ill will produced his injury and the injury caused resentment, then the resentment created anger. Nature has forever abhorred a vacuum, and by the law of attraction, the void his anger created by giving it away caused even more rage to rush in and fill the empty space. He was no different in this than anyone else, but the conflict he endured because of his psychic cowardice made escape an absolute necessity. The bottle was his lifeboat away from the sinking ship of fools. The message in his bottle was that he would never sink, as long as he remained inside it.

He wondered where God was and where he had been when he needed Him. He couldn't understand that God had been there all along. God appeared but was denied. He was the dread, the fear, the guilt and the good people. They were the lifelines he had pushed away. God tried to tell him that the spot he considered so valuable was not really sweet at all. It was saccharine. It was artificial, and always was so. But he preferred an artificial sweetness to a tart reality.

He was better off in this place, he thought, than way back when, in who knows where. All the silences that covered the guilt were but a prelude to what had followed. First, the little fibs were convenient. Then the big lies became a necessity. Concealment became not only a way of life, but a desperate attempt to avoid death. It was a slow and painful torture that accompanied every hour of abstinence. The flights to the hidden stockpile grew more and more frequent as the torture grew less and less bearable.

He remembered those days, and though they had almost faded to black, he experienced his final moment of clarity. He no longer had to hide what he was. It was there for all to see; the sunken cheekbones and the grizzled features, the ragged clothes and the rotting teeth, the shaking hands and the emaciated frame. And why shouldn't all the evidence of his squandered life be on display? He was not in hiding. He knew that he could have made different choices, just like the one he was now making. He might have made it, had he the will to do so.

He headed back to his hovel later that afternoon, armed with a kings ransom. Even if he was just a king of the road. Two inebriated hours later, amidst a crippling traffic jam, his proof of God arrived as mannah from heaven. A tractor-trailer had overturned, right at the top of his offramp. Cases and cases of little plastic bottles destined for various pharmacies fell off the truck and landed in the brush that was his front yard, backyard and scenic view. 90% isopropyl alcohol was written on the labels. Would he make his biblical Exodus? He didn't know, but it was obvious to him right then and there that the existence of heaven was a 90% probability.

Henry started his trip north on Interstate 55 at about one o'clock on Monday afternoon. This was only the second time he'd taken his new top-of-the-line fifth wheel for an elongated spin. The first time he had to convince Charlene it wasn't really like camping at all. She never actually liked it very much, but with her own toilet and shower, it was at least bearable. She couldn't understand what all the fuss was about when it came to camping.

Henry explained to her that he wanted to travel all of North America, in style, ever since he read John Steinbeck's book, 'In Search Of America'. That was Steinbeck's account of his travels with Charley, his little dog and traveling companion. He said he loved that book. It opened his eyes to the wide-open spaces and miles of roads just waiting to be experienced. Where Steinbeck had limited his journey to the continental United States, Henry planned to include Canada as well. It was to be a voyage of personal discovery, he said. When he would find the time to do it was anybody's guess.

This week's trip though, was one of a more grave nature. He was headed for Youngstown, New York. There were sites to see there, but his sites were set on something a little less historic than an old fort. He

The Skater

allotted himself twenty-four hours, or thereabouts, to make the trip from Baton Rouge to Darien Lake, where he intended to leave his trailer before driving to Youngstown.

His brain had never fired off so many neurons in his life as it had done in the last twenty-four hours. Everything would need to be moved ahead now, his investment scam, his relocation to Grand Cayman, everything. His Vegas betting scheme couldn't go ahead the way he'd originally intended, either. Simon was the pivotal player in his original plan and would be the key man in the new one, but his revised idea promised a much smaller payoff. His investment deal still might pay off handsomely if the four dolts took the bait he'd just sent them.

His own original idea for Simon and the team was hatched from nothing more than sheer malice and greed. Having Charlene in his camp was good cover for the drugs he was going to administer to a few key players. A lot of money, billions in fact, was wagered on the Super Bowl and the playoffs leading up to it. As long as the team made the playoffs, he thought, he would make money. If they had the good fortune to get to the Super Bowl, he stood to score a major blow to the casinos. And he was planning to make his money by betting explicitly against the Jaguars.

The drugs figured only minimally in his dream of riches. Some antidepressants here, some antianxiety medications there, and patients were more easily mesmerized. Hypnotic suggestion is a very powerful tool, but in Henry's hands it was positively dominant. He didn't need the theatrics of anyone clucking like a chicken or beying at the moon. He just required some wildly inaccurate fourth-down snaps, some bungled place holding and some flubbed field-goal attempts. Any one of the three would do the trick. Combined with a missed block here or there, critical offsides or penalties, and he'd have the loss that would gift wrap his gain.

He found it very difficult at times not to be smug, because it was so straightforward and uncomplicated for him. The best and most undetectable motive was the one that didn't appear to exist. Or the one that had no rational reason to exist. Operating surreptitiously was his strong suit.

The fake mining exploration deal he sold to the Four Horsemen, which promised a 20% return within six months, was revised. He issued them checks from the 'company' for 30% of their original outlay. And this was only two months later. So, for a $10,000 investment they each received $3000 in less than two months. Never mind that he still had $28,000 of their money in the truck and had only paid them with 30% of their own cash. P.T. Barnum would have been proud, he mused.

He wasn't absolutely certain he could hook them all but even one or two out of four would be okay. The players he was setting up had all signed lucrative contracts that season. The entire team was on a high due to their impressive turnaround, and he figured to capitalize on that. The ten thousand they had each given him was chump change compared to the amounts he was hoping to bilk from them. But there was nothing like success, and when success was happening, both on and off the field, the art of confidence was that much easier.

His skill in manipulating them psychologically was unmatched. He fully realized that his own physical presence, or lack of it, played perfectly into his plans. These guys were big, strong, aggressive alpha males. He, in any other setting, was a puny, weak, submissive sort. Their egos were twice as large as their bodies. How could they ever have allowed themselves to believe, even for a second, that this little man would have the guile, brains and courage to steal their money? If their egos contemplated that, then they would need to accept their own weakness and stupidity. So, denial was imperative for them.

Somewhere around Charlotte he spotted an IHOP. He never tired of their food. He hadn't eaten much all day and he was ravenous. He had actually eaten two bananas and a bag of potato chips, but he didn't consider that to be enough under any circumstances. No, he was ravenous, and a break was a good idea.

As he ate he wondered how quickly he would be able to find Timchuk. He never actually considered that it would take him very long because he trusted himself totally. He knew the locale reasonably well. He had been in that area, around Toronto, a number of times when he was younger. He believed he would find the skater without too much trouble. Money talked. And where he was going his money would talk with a derelict dialect.

An hour later as he continued driving, he thought at great length about how to handle Cameron Timchuk. He must have been at least a little trepidatious because he was thinking both silently and audibly at the same time. He was filling the mostly empty truck cab to capacity with his mental machinations. A while later, when he stopped to get a coffee, he opened his door and it all came swooshing out.

Cameron d'you remember me? No. That's fuckin' stupid. Cameron, long time no see-somethin' like that. Make him think he already knows me. Even if he can't remember. Yeah, long time no... or it's been a while. Get him to remember me. Even if he doesn't, like hypnotic sugg... Too bad couldn't use that. Drunk, never work. Wouldn't remember. Implanted memories. Shit, never know with a piss tank. Skates in the RV. Perfect. Least maybe skates, associate skates... Skating with me. By him lots of booze. Harder the better. Get him to remember my name. Gotta remember my name... might be all I need. Buchanan says my name, he associates with skates... light goes on, might be enough. Might remember I bought him booze. No. Tell him I found booze... or he won a contest. That'd really sound whacked. Guy's in outer space. Can't believe anything. Get him totally legless....

The Skater

drive him to another city. Shit, that's a friggin' good idea...... drop the dirt bag in a different ci...somewhere else. Falls. Across the border, no way, too dangerous. Christ, more time I could drop him in North Bay.

Jesus, that's gorgeous. What fuckin' scenery, that's beautiful. Yeah, okay numbskull...Can see where I'm going you fuckin' asshole.

Maybe a good idea. Lots of places. Drop him... way back. Too bad wouldn't drink himself to death. Get him a room, nah lives on the street. Glad got my skates. Luck. Thanks for teaching me to skate Dad... prick...Probably fuckin' her right now. Scum bucket. Get you, monster faggot. 'll be great. Get you, you cocksucker. You'll pay motherfucker. Henry Collier. Always win... never forget it. You too, squeegee fuck. I decide. You're all nothing. I fucking decide.

It was a good thing it was breezy when he opened the door. That could have hurt somebody passing by.

Henry had much to think about, plans to make and scenarios to consider. His mind continually returned to the idea of dropping Timchuk in another city. Why didn't he think of that before? Did he have the time? All things considered, he didn't think so because he had plans for Simon and Charlene at the end of the week.

For some reason he started humming the old commercial jingle Doris Day used to sing. "See the USA in your Chevrolet." His mother used to sing that now and again when he was small, and they used to laugh about it. He wondered if Doris Day laughed when she found out that the guy she'd been kissing all those years in the movies had AIDS. Probably not, he concluded.

One of the very few normal aspects of Henry's personality was his love of travel. Car travel, especially. It was a funny thing. The only time he felt connected to the world was when he was passing it by. Every sign that indicated a city or town would entice him and he would project himself into living there. He thought he could have been a completely different person in a different city. Maybe he could've had a different occupation. Maybe he could've been a celebrity or a powerful politician, he thought. Whatever his life might have been in any particular place, people would have feared and respected him. That was for sure. He was certain of it.

CHAPTER 13

Deborah Dececchi got interested in the idea of owning a professional sports franchise in the early 90's. Having a son who was a collegiate hockey player and being married to a former NHL scout, she felt a professional hockey franchise would be a good fit. Unfortunately, there was nothing available or appealing in the world of hockey. Though she loved and enjoyed her football team, she always regretted that it couldn't have been a hockey franchise. She always felt that Murray would have flourished much more, had she been the owner of a professional hockey team.

Murray, for his part, couldn't have cared less. He golfed, fished, had plenty to do and yet could still get to a hockey game whenever he wished. He basked in the sunshine of Florida and lived the good life. He had much, much more than he believed he deserved. And since he had it, he wasn't prepared to give it back. Sure, he would have loved to have Deborah along with him more often, but such was his life, he thought. One day, they would have more time for each other, he was sure of it.

"Murray, can I talk to you for a minute?" Deborah asked.

"Sounds serious hun, what's up?"

"I'm thinking of selling."

"Selling? The team?" Murray was caught off guard, and sure didn't see this coming.

"Yeah."

"Why?"

There were lots of little reasons why Deborah was growing weary of ownership. One of the biggest reasons was her recent battle with cancer. She felt very well now, and was in complete remission, but who knew the exact hour or day of one's passing? No one, and she certainly couldn't hazard a guess at hers. Another consideration she pondered was her age. She was seventy-three. She had plenty of energy left but wondered if it would be better spent alongside Murray, enjoying life with the man she loved so dearly.

"I'm tired. I think it's time to enter a new phase. Maybe I'm already in it. I don't know. I'm kind of anxious lately."

"What phase?" Murray asked her.

"The golfing, fishing, puttering phase."

"You sure?"

"You don't want me out on your boat?"

"Of course I do. But do you really want to spend most of your time doing what I like?"

"I like golfing and fishing." It appeared to Murray that Deborah was trying to convince herself.

"Yeah, you love golf. Fishing, not so much."

"So I'll do more golfing and less fishing."

"What about me? Do I do more golfing and less fishing too?"

"Not if you don't want to."

"I want to," Murray said as he knew that, as always, they would work out the logistics. Eventually, he would be splitting his time between golfing and fishing as he wished. And she would be doing the same.

"Great. Maybe we can recapture some of our lost romance?" Deborah laughed.

"Don't get me started on that."

Murray was, to some extent, a thinking man's man. He possessed the rare ability to see what others could not see. He was half joking when he said that to Deborah, but it was something, or one of the many things, he understood differently from others. What he was referring to was the little blue pill syndrome, which seemed to be sweeping the known, civilized world.

In the past, before erection medication, men underwent a psychological catharsis as Father Time's pendulum no longer swung as it used to swing. For a great many fellows, himself included, it was a period of considerable spiritual and philosophical growth. It was a time to appreciate beauty for its own sake and not because of a desire to hop in the sack with it. It was a time to experience life on its own terms, not to push an agenda or drive a lust. It was a time to be accessible and receptive, not unresponsive and narrow-minded. As the body slowed and sensibilities changed, the soul seemed to grow as desires seemed to delay.

Murray held that the prevalence of this new tumescence tablet was not a panacea. While a godsend to anyone suffering from impotence, he felt its widespread use would put untold pressure on men who would otherwise be entering a burgeoning phase of spiritual enlightenment. It would elicit unnecessary temptation as the 'studly' wannabes actually could be, once again. They would feel they could recapture their lost youth. But their youth wasn't lost. It had grown into something else, something older. And anything worthwhile and worth having, he thought, should be left free and not captured.

Deborah understood his incisive and fiercely honest sense of justice. Many of her friends, though, did not. In fact, a few of their friends considered Murray a misogynist. He went to great lengths in detailing why they should consider him to be, simply, their polar opposite. They were feminists, and he was a masculinist. It was that simple to Murray, but he and Deborah appeared to be the only ones who got it.

He viewed the new era, with all its advances in science and technology, as both a curse and a blessing. It was a blessing for all the obvious reasons. It was a curse for impeding the natural flow of life as it had hitherto always existed. As a prime example, he cited the little blue pill syndrome and the unintended consequences that could occur for someone willingly afflicted with LBPS.

In the natural order of life, before the advent of 'chemical hydraulics', Murray contended that men, having the more forceful sex drive, were stymied a good percentage of the time. Their wives, girlfriends or other partners had many good excuses and provided many good reasons why sex was not possible or necessary at any given time. What was the result? Decent men gave up and did without. What happened was what happens in any civilized society, he said. The women were in control of the level of sexual activity in any healthy relationship. This situation curbed male lust. Men just had to deal with that. As couples grew older, women had to deal with the same predicament of not having sex when they wanted it. And at that point, their lust was being curtailed for a good reason too.

Murray saw a perfect natural justice in this. He also saw that, with the help of medicine and perhaps contrary to their new sensibilities, men were once again living in a civilized sexual subservience. The natural laws were being circumvented, he thought. Women would normally have had to accept and deal with the frustrations just as the men had been forced to do. Now, however, that was not likely. And one of the great lessons in life was denied women, while the great spiritual emancipation men sought was denied them.

So when Murray said, "Don't get me started on that," he really meant it. But spending more time with Deborah was something he had been joyfully anticipating for a long time.

It was just as well Henry didn't know anything about her thoughts on selling the team. In fact, no one knew, and no one would know for quite a while. But had he known, he probably would have tried to put together some harebrained scheme to take over the team.

Henry was still driving. He phoned ahead only to discover that Six Flags Darien Lake wasn't open at that time in October. Revising his plans, he found a campsite still open in Youngstown. That was good, because it was from Youngstown that he planned to cross the border into Canada.

The next time he stopped for gas, he picked up the latest local edition of the Boat Trader. He found a few possible purchases to consider. Of course, he needed to factor in exactly where the boat was being sold. He didn't want to go too far out of his way to get it. He didn't have the time. He wasn't certain whether he should buy a little old thing or something more befitting his taste. After all, he liked his toys.

He wasn't going to cross into Canada in his truck. That would have been stupid. He would use an American boat to cross. He planned to use the cover of darkness. He didn't expect to encounter any Canadian authorities on the way over. On the way back he would deal with whatever arose when the time came. At least he had all his ID in order. His boat would be American, and filled with nothing more than an old pair of skates and maybe a fish or two.

Nobody would ever know that he left the US and entered Canada. That was his plan. How could he have had anything to do with Cam Timchuk's disappearance, or in any way influenced his memory, if he had never been in the country in the first place?

Sometimes when Henry considered alternate occupations, and that was usually when he was driving, he thought about working covertly for the CIA or the FBI. He knew himself well enough to understand that he was already operating covertly in his own life. It was his life, his entire life. He never did anything without the most selfish ulterior motives. That's why he was convinced that there never was a person born who could have made a better spy than he already was.

From infancy, he was trained. At first he just tiptoed around his father but he soon learned, as he grew, that stealth would be his constant companion, if he were to survive. With the tacit approval of his mother, he began to thrive in his deprivation. His father never nurtured him. He mostly disregarded him, but his mother gave her silent approval for Henry's ever increasing slyness. It was she who bequeathed her psychic persona to him, not his father.

He was an ungrateful yet prolific beneficiary. It would have been easy for anyone to misinterpret his mother's motives but she was trying to protect him, in a sense. If Henry had not become the cunning manipulator she encouraged him to be, he would probably have been institutionalized. Or, at the very least, a depressed and heavily medicated victim. She wasn't going to raise a loser like her husband. She succeeded where medicine would surely have failed. Her son was a user, not a loser; a winner, not

The Skater

a whiner; and while her husband had almost been a pro, her son would definitely be a con.

He didn't think about his mother very often, but at this moment in time he did. He knew if she had not been his mother he wouldn't have liked her very much. He also knew the feeling was mutual, but they both had a grudging respect for one another. She respected Henry for making it. He respected her for making him. He cast his mind back to all the times his mother intervened on his behalf, protecting him from the old man's wrath.

Now, she was in Aruba, and he wished her well and hoped she was enjoying herself. She deserved the highlife as much as he did. The one thing they had in common was enough to forge a distant and tenuous bond. They were both survivors. He remembered the day his father finally died. The first words out of his mouth were, "the reign of terror is over." The first words out of Edith's mouth were, "I finally did it."

Were it not for a clerical error at the local drugstore, Edith might never have had the idea or the means to plot her husband's last hurrah and final 'closing time'. On the one hand, the clerical error made by Cynthia Ramos gave Edith the little impetus she needed to conceive Johnny's final 'bender'. On the other hand, Ms. Ramos' error prolonged the lifespan of Johnny Collier and extended the cause of his death, much to Edith's chagrin.

Reed's pharmacy was a family-run operation. It was entrenched in the local community for well over forty years. It changed ownership twice in that time. The current owner, Jim Van Brummel, thought the time had come to accept the corporate purchase that was inevitable. Two months down the road his pharmacy would be absorbed into a national chain. So, he was busily trying to reduce his stock when Ms. Ramos made her error. Instead of ordering a gross of rubbing alcohol bottles, she ordered a gross of cases. All this happened when Van Brummel was on vacation. By the time he returned, his assistant had mistakenly paid the invoice, and he was stuck with the extra inventory.

In an effort to clean out most of his stock, everything in the store was drastically reduced. It was precisely because it was on sale at an unbelievably low price that Edith Collier hatched her plan to assist her husband's passing. It was something she found quite funny when she realized that her terminally ill husband would have her help in an 'assisted homicide'. She purchased cases and cases of the rubbing alcohol, and at every opportunity she spiked her husband's booze.

When he went to the toilet and left a half finished bottle of beer on the table, she would pour alcohol in it. When he was a third to half way through a forty ouncer, she would add rubbing alcohol. Wine, liqueur and cider were all fair game. Johnny couldn't figure it out. He was getting drunker faster than ever before. He had no reason to dwell on it anyway, because he was the unwitting heir to this fortified scotch throne. He couldn't believe his luck. The booze seemed to last longer and longer and he felt like he had won the lottery.

Edith's displeasure arose from the knowledge that Ms. Ramos had actually made two mistakes when she ordered the gross of rubbing alcohol. She helped Edith by providing the liquid murder weapon, but she also hindered her by diluting it, so to speak. Unlike Cameron Timchuk's 90% solution, Cynthia Ramos ordered a 70% solution, which gave Johnny Collier an extra few weeks on the planet to be spaced out, before he really and truly would be.

Henry was amused that his mother was finally taking a well-deserved rest, drinking heavily and sleeping lightly, no doubt. It slipped his mind, where she told him she had hidden her emergency key. She only ever told him once, but he was fairly certain it was at the top of the downspout in the eaves trough, on top of the wire mesh leaf catcher at the northeast corner of the house. When he thought about it, he smirked. He knew he had to be right. That was far too specific a memory to be a random guess. And what an ingenious hiding spot, he thought.

She was as ingenious as she was devious. He remembered all the times his mother stole money from his father. She only did it when his father was three sheets to the wind and completely incapable of noticing or remembering. He never told his mother that he saw her, because he didn't want her to know the extent of his omniscience. If she knew that Henry was aware of her thievery, then in his mind, his omniscience would be compromised. The proof of his own theory was unknown to him, because his mother always wanted him to know what she was doing.

She had always been ambitious to turn him into a master manipulator. She grew tired of her own molded existence, shaped by the failures of her husband. She reasoned that living vicariously through her son was infinitely preferable to the lingering psychological death she was enduring. She was certain that she was the sole controller of his experiences and interpretations. She marginalized her husband's influence over her son so that his only impact on the boy was negative. The more negative his influence was, the more dominating hers became.

While Henry thought he was king of the world, he only ascended to the throne by the abdication of his mother, the Queen. He wasn't conscious of the Queen's commission of regicide, which ultimately ended the reign of terror from which he was so relieved to emerge. His mental predisposition toward secrecy and away from judgment was either inherited or created, or both. In any case, his mother was the cause. Their fear of judgment drove them both to seek comfort in secrecy. In this they were identical.

The Skater

The King, pulled by 500 horses, felt resplendent in his big black carriage amidst other highwaymen as he journeyed toward old Fort Niagara. It was a bright and beautiful autumn day filled with both promise and reward. He relished overcoming difficulties and undermining authority. To him, this was a great adventure, and in the end the King would decree the fate of his subject. In the royal court of his mind, he listened to the advice of his knights and chancellors, telling them that he would retire to his quarters when they reached the fort. There, he would make his decision. One of three fates awaited his subject. King Henry would issue his proclamation of exile, extortion or execution.

All the thinking about his mother stirred his memory of Nancy. He remembered the night his sister was killed, and how distraught his mother was. It happened on a Friday. Edith kept Nancy home from school Thursday and Friday because she seemed to be coming down with the flu. Johnny was on day shift, but hadn't come home from work. He was in the hotel, as usual for a Friday night. He made his incoherent phone call home at about midnight. This was earlier than he usually called, so Edith knew he'd run out of money.

Edith had two doctor's appointments that day, one of which she couldn't cancel. So, with Nancy not in school she persuaded Johnny to let her drive him to work. That way she could keep her appointments and take care of Nancy. She promised to collect him after work, which actually meant near closing time. She only made that deal with him because she had to keep that appointment.

When the phone rang, she was nodding off to the news. She tried to convince Johnny to get a cab, but he had no money left, and she did make the deal to pick him up. So, she reluctantly agreed. The phone woke Nancy up. She was crying because her throat was sore. Henry was already in bed so she just bundled up her daughter and took her along. It was only a fifteen minute trip, there and back. Henry would never know he was alone, and Nancy would probably be asleep by the time they got back home, she reasoned.

The accident happened on their way home from the hotel. Johnny fell asleep in the backseat. Nancy occupied the front passenger seat. Edith always made sure she buckled her seat belt. Nancy wanted to cuddle up to her mom and sprawl across her lap but Edith made her sit in the passenger seat and buckle up. For safety's sake.

She never had a chance. A drunk in a pickup truck broadsided them, crashing into the front passenger side of the car at an intersection about one minute from home. She was killed instantly. Edith broke her arm and collarbone. Johnny suffered only a headache, from the impact of his head hitting the door.

Edith blamed herself and the drunk driver, but mostly, she blamed the drunk in the back of the car. It should've been him driving home alone in the car, she thought. It should've been him who was killed. Her precious daughter was gone and her worthless husband wasn't. She vowed to get even. She didn't know how she would do it, but she knew that somehow, someway, she would make it happen.

So when the drugstore inspired and tempted her with their super sale, she took the opportunity and fulfilled her vow. He was rapidly drinking himself to death anyway. She was just helping him along and she knew, with his well documented and advanced liver condition, no one would suspect anything other than self-inflicted death by alcoholism. She was right. But just to be safe, she made sure to hide all the cases and bottles before she called 911.

Henry drove into the campsite at about 1:30 PM on Tuesday afternoon. He told the attendant he would be leaving the next day by noon, or at the latest one o'clock. The lady informed him that he would have to pay for two days because of their check-in and checkout rules. Henry argued with the woman for a couple of minutes, basing his complaint on the fact that he wouldn't be in the campsite for a full twenty-four hours. "Why would you charge me for two days?"

He relented finally and handed her his credit card. He wasn't concerned about the two-day charge at all. He just wanted this woman to remember him. His entire journey north and back down south again was, and would be, well documented. The illegal border crossing would not be so well documented. If all went well it would be completely under the radar.

He parked, unhooked and then made all the appropriate hookups. His pickup was now free. He set his little traveling windup alarm clock for 3:30 PM and fell asleep instantly when his head met the mattress. He slept soundly and dreamt furiously.

He woke to the old world sound of an old-fashioned alarm bell. The first thing he did was call Sam. That was the name of the guy selling the boat. He wanted $4000 or best offer. Sam didn't know it yet, but he would get the best offer he could ever imagine.

Sam lived about ten minutes away from the campsite. Henry said he'd be at his place in thirty minutes. Sam told him it was an older boat, but in good condition. It was good for fishing or cruising and the engine was in good shape. He told Henry about the horsepower, but he didn't listen because he was thinking only about Cameron Timchuk. Sam even said there was a full tank of gas in it. Henry certainly heard that as he read through the listing again. It said the boat was a 1980 ASI Imperial Tri Hull Bowrider. It was 15 1/2 feet long and came with a trailer and a 75 hp engine. It sounded good to him.

The Skater

"How many miles will I get out of a full tank, cruising?"
" I don't know.Maybe a hundred?" Sam said.
"You're asking four thousand with the trailer, right?"
"Yep."
"Okay. I'll be there in about half an hour. How do I get there from here?"

Sam gave him directions, and that was that. Henry finished the bag of potato chips he started when he got to the campground. He washed his face, brushed his teeth and combed his hair. He threw on a clean shirt and gathered up his gear, which included his father's skates and his old Ontario license plates, all stuffed in his backpack.

When he got to Sam's place the boat was on the left side of the double wide driveway. It looked all right to Henry, but he didn't know too much about boats. The important thing was, he knew how to steer it. And he knew where he was going.

Sam met him on the port side of the boat in the middle of the driveway. Henry guessed Sam's age to be about seventy-five. He struggled to walk and appeared out of breath as he spoke. He told him it was his brother's boat, and that his brother died a couple of months ago. He was the only sibling left now, he said. He told Henry his neighbor, three doors down, wanted it but he wasn't prepared to give him any more than $3500 for it. Sam knew it was worth $4000, and he sure wasn't going to give it away.

Henry agreed. He said it looked to be in pretty good shape, and he asked how long it had been since it was in the water.

"July 4th weekend. Joe took his great-grandson out for a little cruise to celebrate. That was the last time he ever took it out. Three weeks later he had a heart attack and died right there at breakfast."

"Sorry. Sam, I think I'm going to make you an offer you can't refuse." Henry was surprised at what he said and how he felt right in that moment. He was going to get his way, as usual, and he was going to help this old guy a little bit too. He wasn't entirely altruistic though, because as always, he had his motives.

"I can't go below $3500."

"Sam, you don't have to go below your asking price at all. Not one penny." As he said that Henry reached into his pocket, as planned, and pulled out his checkbook. He fumbled a few seconds to let Sam absorb the situation. Even an honest old guy like Sam would balk at accepting an uncertified check from a stranger. Henry looked at him and asked him if he had a pen.

"Look, uh, I don't want to seem rude but... would you accept a check from a stranger? Uncertified?"

"You know what, you're right. You've got no idea who I am." And Henry really meant that. "It's just that you said your neighbor's interested and I figured, you know, if he changes his mind and decides to up the ante I'll lose my chance to buy it from you."

"I don't think that's going to happen anytime soon."

"Well, you know what they say, he who hesitates is lost. Look, is there a bank around here?" Henry asked.

"You passed one coming here. The mall around the corner."

Henry hurried to his truck, opened the door and pulled out his wallet, which was lying on the front passenger seat. He made sure to let Sam see him counting out five twenty dollar bills. He put the wallet back on the seat, closed the door and walked back to meet Sam, extending the hundred bucks to him. Sam had a puzzled look on his face. "That's just your holding fee. So you don't go and sell this beauty to your neighbor, before I get back with the cash. That is what you'd prefer, right? Cash?"

"Yeah, cash is good."

"What bank is it? 'Cause I usually bank at Marine Midland when I'm up this way."

"Yeah, it's a Marine Midland. Tucked in the corner of the mall. Not surprised you didn't see it," Sam said.

"No. I didn't," Henry lied.

So, off Henry went around the corner to buy a coffee at the Starbucks he also didn't notice. He drank half of his coffee, no sugar, and then headed back to Sam's place. He had lots of cash in his truck, courtesy of the four chumps in Jacksonville. He knew how it would have looked to Sam if he had just reached into his truck and pulled out the money. All the world's a stage. And he couldn't have staged it any better.

He handed over $6000 to Sam, who was incredulous as Henry counted it out. "It's only four thousand," Sam pleaded.

"I know Sam, but here's the offer I'm going to make you. I only need the boat for one day. I know it sounds crazy, but I'm proposing to my fiancé tonight. And I need to do it on a boat. It's a long story, but it has to be out on the water. She's gonna love it. I know it," Henry said.

"Congratulations. Sure seems like you're goin' to a lot of trouble."

"Nothin' but the best for my Bobby Jo. Anyway, so here's my offer to you. If she likes the boat, and I know she will, you've got your $6000, and we've got our boat. If she doesn't like it, and I can't see that happening, we'll bring your boat back tomorrow."

"And I give you your money back, is that it?"

"No. You give me four thousand back. You keep two thousand for renting me your boat and helping me propose to Bobby Jo."

"Let me get this straight. Do I give you a bill of sale?" Sam was getting a little confused.

The Skater

"Of course. You're selling me your boat, but if I have to come back tomorrow you've just rented it to us. I'll give you the receipt back. You keep two grand for your kindness and give me the other four back."

"What if I don't want to give you the other four back?"

"Then I keep your boat."

"I see," Sam said, suppressing a grin.

Sam knew he couldn't lose, and Henry didn't have to help him understand that he was holding all the cards. He knew he could get $3500 from his neighbor. But right now, he had $6100 in his hands. He saw that if he took the boat back from Henry tomorrow, he would have $2100, and the boat, which he could sell to his neighbor for $3500. He could make $1600 more than the boat was worth by doing the fair thing. He could make $2100 more than it was worth by not playing fair and not taking the boat back from Henry. Well, Henry and Bobby Jo.

This was the first hustle Henry ever perpetrated that didn't result in a victim being scammed. In fact, Henry was the one losing money this time, but it was well worth it. It wasn't his money anyway, so he didn't care. As far as Sam was involved, Henry's good deed was only done to facilitate a bad one. And he knew Sam would take the boat back.

Sam took him through the back door into the kitchen and there he wrote a bill of sale for $4000. If the boat stayed in Henry's possession he'd only have to worry about sales tax on $4000, and if he took it back he'd tear up the receipt and pocket two thousand dollars, tax-free. With that, Henry left the house and began hitching up the boat and trailer. He was gone in less than five minutes. Sam stood in the driveway wishing him the best of luck. Henry waved out the window and showed his crossed fingers as he drove away.

First things first, he thought, as he poked his way through listings on his GPS looking for a local IHOP. The closest IHOP was in Amherst, which was about thirty minutes away. It was almost five o'clock when he started out. At 5:30 PM, he walked through the door of the restaurant. By seven o'clock the boat was in the water, and the truck was parked back up in the paved lot beside the ramp.

He sailed out slowly from the mouth of the Niagara River bearing north northeast into Lake Ontario. He stayed in US waters until it was dark enough to turn west, cross the border, and head to his mother's house. Edith's property backed onto the south shore of Lake Ontario. The new breakwall and dock she installed wasn't cheap, but the rate she was selling real estate at made it real easy to pay for.

He calculated it would take him about forty-five minutes to cruise to his mother's place. There was some moonlight but it appeared only sporadically due to the cloud cover. Sam had graciously given him a fishing rod and a little tackle and bait starter kit. He thought to do a little fishing, maybe tomorrow. For now, he was content to steer his small vessel, make sure he didn't hit a sand bar and stay clear of the Canadian Forces Base firing range, which extended out into the lake. It was marked with buoys, but he wasn't positive he would even be able to see them when the moon was hidden.

He felt surprisingly invigorated just by being out on the water, and he felt in total control of the boat. It was very important for him to be in control. He was in control only as long as he was under control. And that was usually where he was.

The excitement was building in him. He knew he was now in the middle of perpetrating something magnificent, a black op, a clandestine and covert secret attack, behind enemy lines and beyond the reach of the law. He experienced his Great Lakes epiphany in an anxious and exhilarated frame of mind. He knew his life would never and could never be the same after this. He was also certain he was born to do this, whatever 'this' was. The anticipation, the adrenaline and the rush were intoxicating him. It wasn't just a mental high either. He felt a naked sexual arousal too. He was awakened to the realization that there would never, ever be another feeling like it. Unless he was prepared to leap enthusiastically off the cliffs of normality into the gorge of depravity. All things considered, Henry thought of himself as a pretty good jumper.

The boat crossing from Youngstown to Niagara-on-the-Lake went completely without incident. He spotted his mother's new dock easily. Although he had never been to her new home before, her new dock was easy to spot. It was brightly lit, with the name EDITH traced across the face of a stone wall above the break wall. His mother was an unashamed advertiser for herself. In the local real estate industry that was how she advertised herself, simply as Edith. And everyone knew who she was. "Thanks mom," Henry said as he docked his boat and tied it off.

It was a large lot, roughly three acres from the water's edge to the house on the Firelane. Walking up the steps and out onto the grass behind the stone wall, Henry surveyed the property. He noticed first the high fence running down both sides of the property all the way to what would have been the original water's edge but was now a fortified breakwall, with the stairwell running down to the dock. Right beside the dock was the boat ramp, which wasn't yet paved.

Henry approached the house from the north. The key should be in the eaves trough at the left-hand corner, he thought. He was right, but a little bemused as to how best to climb up to get it. The little shed was locked, as was the detached garage and the boathouse. He checked under the cedar deck, happy to see a ladder. As luck would have it, the ladder was an old, not too sturdy, orchard ladder. He didn't have to shinny up the old TV antenna pole, and he was relieved about that. The key was right where his mother said it would be but a little slimy from all the rain and leaves and bird shit. He wiped it as best he could and slid it into his pocket, leaving remnants of leafy bird feces on his shirt and pants.

As he entered the side door into a small vestibule, he expected to hear the security alarm go off. It didn't. The security system was accidentally disabled during the movement of equipment in his mother's driveway when the new breakwall was being installed. Edith left a note for herself, to call the security company when she returned from Aruba. Henry's luck continued.

He walked around, investigating, inhaling and snooping. He wondered if his mother had a secret stash of drugs or pornography. Did she have a boyfriend? That was the next thought to cross his mind. The walk-in closet in her bedroom answered that question. No, she didn't have a boyfriend. She had a girlfriend.

He wasn't surprised at his discovery. How could someone who'd gone through and endured what she had endured ever trust a man again? She needed warmth and tenderness. She needed to feel safe and secure, something that eluded her for nearly twenty five years of her life. Judging by the two business cards on the right-hand night table, her girlfriend was Meena Khan, barrister and solicitor. "Bare assed her and solicit her, couldn't have done better myself, mom."

The car keys for two vehicles were hanging by the door into the attached garage. He opened the door to sneak a peek at what he was choosing between. A beautiful silver BMW and a red Ford pickup truck were facing him. He took the keys to the pickup truck, entered the garage, opened the driver's door and threw his backpack, laptop and stolen bottle of scotch on the seat. He found a screwdriver on the old kitchen countertop, which had been moved to the garage when his mother remodeled. He removed the plates and threw them onto the countertop. He fastened his own old Ontario plates to the vehicle. The only thing left for him to do was remove the sticker from his mother's back plate. He managed to pull it off, but took with it two previous years stickers as well. His little tube of crazy glue did the rest.

He climbed into the truck and closed the door. First, he tested the garage door opener a couple of times. Second, he checked the fuel gauge. "Another full tank of gas. I can't fuckin' believe it."

On the drive to the big city he couldn't help feeling he was a pariah. He was an outlaw, for sure. He was an illegal alien, because he entered the country unlawfully and illegally. However, he was still a Canadian citizen. So, what exactly was he? They couldn't deport him to the United States.

He only had a green card. He was in a very interesting situation and if he were to be intercepted by the authorities, what then? Probably nothing, he reasoned. But he had no intention of running afoul of the law.

He took the slower, more congested route. He stayed on the QEW all the way rather than travel the 407, which would have been quicker. The 407 had an automated toll system, and Henry certainly didn't need his old Ontario plates being photographed. He changed the P to a B a long time ago, but there was no point in pushing his luck.

Arriving in the city around midnight, the first doubt crept up on him. How would he be able to make any meaningful inquiries at this time of night? Going directly to the homeless shelters seemed the most direct way to glean some information. He thought about impersonating Timchuk's brother. Yes, that's what he would do, he thought.

The one thing Henry didn't have on his side was the weather. It was unseasonably warm for October. Any down and out street drunk, worth his salt in these northern climes, would never have slept inside. So, he wasn't likely to find him at a shelter. Nonetheless, he needed to start somewhere. He googled shelters in the city, made a list, and started with the Salvation Army. He had no luck there. The second shelter he went to looked to be slightly seedier than the Sally Ann. The night warden, as Henry thought of him, claimed to know who he was asking about. He said there was an old fellow on the other side of the room he could talk to. He was on the bed, over in the corner. "Go talk to him yourself."

The place reeked of excreted alcohol. The acrid stench of it nearly made Henry sick, and he was rapidly approaching his gag threshold. Nevertheless, he strode over to the low narrow cot. The man smelled like he was putrefying in a vat of urine and stools. He stank like an un-wiped ass, and he looked dirtier than a pig in slop. Henry had a pungent vision of what a hundred pounds of rancid pork would smell like. Not wanting to, but having to, he prodded the old wheezing geezer in the shoulder. No sign of life. He poked him again, a little more forcefully and then it started. The ancient vagrant began coughing, farting and fumbling as he slobbered his way to consciousness stammering, "wha...wha."

"Sir, can I speak to you for a minute? I'm looking for my brother."

"Brother, you're not my brother," Stinkman said.

"No, my brother. Cam Timchuk's my brother."

"Not my brother either," said Stenchman.

"No. I'm looking for MY brother. Do you know where he is?"

"Who?"

"Cam Timchuk. My brother. Do you know where he is?"

"Dunno. Got any money?"

"Do you mean you don't know where he is? Or you don't know him?"

The Skater

"How can I know where he is, if I don't know 'im?" The old man was really starting to infuriate Henry. It was his father all over again, he thought.

"He was a figure skater. Cameron Timchuk. Ever heard of him?"

"Pansies. Figure skatin.'" The old drunk was fading fast and becoming less coherent with every second.

"Figure skatin' pansies. Yeah. My brother's a figure skatin' pansy. Do you know where he is?"

"Yur brother? Timmy?"

"Yeah, Timmy. My brother. Know where he is?"

"D'ya say ya got money?"

"Sure. Fifty bucks. Know where he is? Timmy?"

If there was one situation Henry had difficulty with, it was talking to someone who was inebriated. Anyone would have thought that with all his experience dealing with his drunken father, he, of all people, would have been able to navigate through the nonsense easily. It wasn't so much a problem of ferreting out the truth. It was restraining himself from lashing out at his father by proxy. He hated people who were drunk. Unless, he was the drunk. It was part and parcel of what he was, what he was becoming. He really wasn't too sure what he was becoming. All he did know was that this vile old man had something he wanted and he wanted it right away or he was going to hurl the remnants of his IHOP platter straight into his beard.

"Yep," he said.

"Where is he then? I have to find him."

"Moved."

"Where'd he move to?"

"Dunno....uh...ol' off-ramp York Mills. Maybe."

"Off-ramp? Where?" Henry was getting very agitated.

"Domfally."

He went back to the warden at the front of the place and asked him if he knew anything about the location. He told Henry he was probably talking about the Don Valley Parkway. He said he didn't know anything about an old ramp, but there was an exit there at York Mills Road. "Thanks," he said and with that, Henry left.

Except for the annoying voice on the GPS, Henry liked it and used it a lot. Especially for locating the nearest IHOP franchise. He wasn't going to find any of those in Toronto. Right now, he was looking for the junction where Timchuk might be located. He found the Don Valley Parkway, where the Gardiner Expressway ended and proceeded north to York Mills Road. He parked his car in a lot a few hundred yards from the ramp. Pulling on his backpack, he grabbed the flashlight from the backseat, locked the truck and started walking into the darkness. He wasn't going to use the flashlight until he was well concealed in the overgrowth of thicket and weeds amidst the trees.

The whoosh of the passing traffic on the DVP was greatly muffled, once he found himself ensconced in the vegetation. After ten or fifteen minutes, he stumbled, literally, on some old ripped up concrete. Upon further inspection, he saw the outline of a curb in the wide bright triangle from his flashlight. Moving toward it, he could see what he thought was an old road. It was definitely pavement, and there was a faded yellow line running down the side of it. The disgusting old man was right. It sure looked to be an old off-ramp or on-ramp. Henry couldn't tell and didn't care.

This was a black op at its finest. He felt his entire life; boyhood, youth, adulthood, was just a training exercise, a prelude to this moment. His heart hammered. His chest felt incredibly congested, like it was going to explode. His breathing grew rapid and shallow. His legs seemed flimsy yet heavy and his hands were quivering. If he had spoken at that moment, he would have sounded like someone who inhaled helium. He had never felt this alive and afraid in his life. This was even better than the feeling he had on the boat crossing. For a moment, the pounding in his ears drowned out the noise of traffic. This feeling he was experiencing was almost more than he could deal with, standing erect. This was more than elation. He preferred this feeling to any orgasm he'd ever experienced. And the best thing was, nobody knew. Nobody knew he was in the country. Nobody knew what he was about to do. And nobody knew the intensity of his excitement.

He aimed the flashlight and saw a small clearing. Bouncing back at him from all around the clearing was a shiny glare. He moved in to investigate.

"Cam Timchuk?" he called out.

"Fuckoff. Y'ain't gettin' any."

"No, I just want to talk to you."

"'Bout what?"

"Your career. Figure skating career."

"What career? It's over, man."

"Listen, I'm a reporter. My name is Jon Buchanan. I work for Skating Life."

"Never heard of it." Cam said.

"We're a new magazine out of Minnesota. My editor said I can pay you $1000 for an interview."

"Yeah? Where's the money?"

Henry pulled ten paper clipped $100 bills out of his pocket. While Cam stared at the money he extracted the big bottle of scotch from the backpack. Now he had Timchuk's attention. He intended to give him the scotch long before he'd hand over any money. The guy was barely compos mentis now, and Henry knew the scotch should be enough to send him

The Skater

to never never land. Judging by the dozens and dozens of empty plastic bottles, Henry wondered how he managed to survive at all. "Peace offering," he said, handing him the bottle.

Cam started chugging like Thomas the Tanked Engineer. He offered Henry a swig of what was now, clearly, bottleneck trench mouth. He declined and encouraged Cam to have it all. "So, Cameron, did you ever have a sports psychologist work with you when you skated?"

"Sporsikolijisz?"

"Yeah."

"Nahh. Never."

"Sure? Guy called Henry Collier? Helped you motivate yourself?"

"Never."

"Think hard now. Are you sure you didn't have a performance guy, a sports motivator? Once, a long time ago?"

"Nope."

Cam continued drinking and with every swallow became more and more incoherent. Within twenty minutes he was two thirds of the way through the bottle. Henry couldn't understand why he was still alive, never mind still awake. He thought Cam was over enjoying the taste of the scotch after drinking all that rubbing alcohol. That was good for Henry.

He took the skates out of the backpack and showed them to Cameron. He wasn't impressed, he could barely focus, but he wasn't impressed.

"Hockey. Shitty skaters."

"These were my dad's skates."

With that, Cameron Timchuk dropped the bottle of scotch onto the ground, and the little left in it slowly trickled out until only a few ounces remained. He fell over in a heap, half on his left side, with his left arm bent at a 90° angle beside his head. His right hand came to rest on the front of his piss stained pants, clenched over his dormant genitals.

For some reason, Henry couldn't get the word 'rubby' out of his mind. He wondered where the word came from. Perhaps it was derived from rubbing alcohol, he thought. He decided that when he had the time he would try to discover the roots of the word. At that moment, the word itself became unreasonably important to him, out of all proportion, considering what he was about to do.

He gazed at the outline of Cameron Timchuk in the dark. "What a waste," he said, shaking his head at the very idea that someone so talented and so young could end up here in the middle of the bush. Just a stone's throw away from normal folks coming and going from dinner parties, movies and whatever else. There were more than two worlds. Sure, there were the worlds of the haves and the have-nots. But how did they come to be? There were the worlds of wannabes, has-beens, the never was, the didn't care, the Cam Timchuks. He began his journey as a wannabe. Then he became a have, a has-been, a have not and finally, a didn't care. Henry was fully prepared, and in his own mind honored, to send Cameron off to meet his fate in the great never was.

For a small framed man he had very large feet. One size smaller than his father's, they were. With the added volume of a pair of work socks, Johnny's skates fit him fine. They were good skates too, purchased just before his father died. Top-of-the-line, they were. Henry slipped his feet into them and laced them up, first the left and then the right. They felt very comfortable to Henry. He was actually a very good skater even though he wasn't an accomplished hockey player. He voiced the opinion once, to his father, that he would like to try figure skating. The support of his father was not forthcoming. There would be no pansies in Johnny's house, and that was that.

Henry tiptoed over to the useless and motionless body of Cameron. He reached down and picked up the bottle of scotch. "Why not?" he said as he guzzled down the remainder and skated across Cameron's neck.

Cleaning up the skates was easy with all the rubbing alcohol lying around. He used some old newspapers to clean off the blades, wrapping the bloody newsprint in the plastic shrinkwrap that had been torn from the cases. With his shoes back on, he messed up the dirt to obscure the straight blade marks left by the skates. He put everything in the back of the truck, including the empty bottle of scotch. His mother's recycling and garbage collection would take care of those.

It was just past three o'clock in the morning. He ate a couple of muffins and had an iced coffee, drove into a nearby rail commuter parking lot and slept until eight thirty.

When he woke up the sun was shining, the birds were singing, the commuters were commuting and Cameron was stiffening as rigor was setting in. His first stop was a large sports store. They had a skate exchange and willingly accepted them from Henry, who willingly relinquished them. The clerk asked him if he was interested in a new pair for the upcoming season. Henry told him no, he had done all the skating he had to do this year.

About ninety minutes later, he stopped at a large supermarket just off the highway to make a seafood purchase. Surveying the big deep freezer section, he saw plenty of flash frozen, shrink-wrapped, whole fish for sale. He didn't want and certainly couldn't use fillets. He needed something whole, with the head on, that could accept a hook and look like a respectable catch from a boater returning to shore. He walked alongside the freezer aisle staring at the piles of fish. First, he saw halibut, and then salmon, followed by mackerel, and tilapia. Perfect, he thought, a couple of tilapia would look impressive. He rummaged through the pile looking for a couple which weren't too big and fat. He settled on a couple from the middle of the pile that weren't too prize worthy. He paid, returned to his truck and then returned to the highway. He made one more stop on his way.

Back at his mother's house, he entered the garage and parked. He retrieved three plastic shopping bags and put the newspapers and shrink-wrap in one of them and tied a knot in it. This went in the second bag, and that went into the third bag. This bloody trinity of plastic and paper was buried in the middle of a large green garbage bag that had already been tied up, waiting for garbage day. The empty bottle of scotch was thrown into the blue recycling bin with two resident others, amidst empty water bottles and cans of juice, pop and pasta sauce. His mother's license plates went back on her truck and he had to crazy glue the sticker, once again. He put his own old plates in the backpack from which he removed the bottle of scotch he bought at his last stop. He replaced the scotch in the liquor cabinet and locked the side door on his way out. He returned the house key to its spot in the eaves trough and walked back to the dock.

With plenty of gas still in the boat, he cruised north a couple of miles before he turned, bearing east to cross back into US waters. He idled while he tore open the shrink-wrapped fish, using the knife Sam put in his starter kit. The fish were almost completely thawed, thanks to the truck heater. Henry hooked them up to look like a fair but not great catch. He threw the plastic wrapping overboard into the water. That was all, he thought, as he began heading back to Youngstown.

Back at the dock, he tied up the boat and went up to bring his truck and trailer down the ramp. When he had the trailer positioned in the water he shut off the truck. He walked back along the dock, to his boat. There, he saw the customs officer looking at it.

"Hi. How are you?" Henry said.

"How long you been out?"

"Since three or four this morning."

"Your boat?" Agent Gunther asked.

"No. It's my uncle's."

"Citizenship?"

"Canadian. But I have a green card. I live here now." Henry tried to proffer his identification. Everything was in order, but this guy spooked him a little bit.

"Where do you live?"

"Baton Rouge."

"Never been there. Catch anything?"

"I caught a couple, that's all. I'm kind of new to fishing."

"Show me."

At this demand, Henry jumped into the boat, grabbed the two fish, held them up and showed Gunther.

"What are they?"

Henry didn't know anything about fish and he was, for a second or two, scared shitless. "Not sure. Any idea?"

"No. No idea. Just transferred here on Monday. Enjoy your catch," Gunther said.

"Thanks."

And with that, Henry's arsehole finally recovered its pucker. He thought, a few moments ago that he might, just slightly, dump in his denims. It was a damn good thing too, that agent Gunther didn't know anything about fish. Even he would have known you can't catch a saltwater fish in a freshwater lake. Henry made the mistake of picking up two mackerel from the middle of that pile, and he didn't check the labels.

Sam took the boat back just as Henry had predicted. Since he was traveling south past Amherst anyway, he pulled in at the IHOP to put on the feed bag. Something peculiar was happening to Henry. His aloof and supercilious attitude was softening, just as his fear, anxiety and exhilaration were beginning to appear. It seemed that his humanness was surfacing, while his humanity was sinking. He felt most alive only through death. The problem for others was that he really liked the feeling.

CHAPTER 14

Jon was beating himself up over whether to throw caution to the wind and call Pamela. It was already Friday morning and he had managed to refrain from phoning this long. So, why not wait until he flew in tonight, was the question he asked himself. He devised his storyline to be that he was just letting her know what time his plane would arrive, and that he would get in touch with her then. So he phoned her.

"Hello."

"Hello, Pamela? Jon Buchanan here."

"Hi Jon. I thought it might be you. I didn't recognize the area code."

"How are you?"

"Fine, but I've got some bad news for you."

"Bad news?"

"That homeless man you wanted to talk to, Jon, he's dead."

"Dead? What happened?"

"He was murdered sometime late Tuesday night. Or early Wednesday morning. His throat was slit. Looks like he was killed by one of his own. There was a traffic accident on Monday. A tractor-trailer overturned. He ended up with a lot of rubbing alcohol. Cases of it. Looks like that's why he was killed, probably a fight over the rubbing alcohol."

"Jesus."

"What time does your plane get in?"

"Gee, uh, I don't see the point now," Jon was sounding quite deflated. All of a sudden, he didn't feel like catching a plane and wasting his time.

"You mean, there is no other reason you'd want to come up for the weekend? No reason at all?"

"Well, come to think of it, yeah. There is another reason. And I thought you were hard to get."

"Yes, I am hard to get but once I'm got......"

"My plane should be in at 10:15 PM."

"Great. I'm off at seven. I bought you something. On a whim. Hope you like it," Pamela said.

"I'm really, really looking forward to seeing you, Pamela."

"I know. Me too. See you tonight."

Charlene met Simon at the airport late Friday afternoon. She didn't tell anyone where she was going or who she was meeting. She and Simon were 'undercover lovers' and probably would remain so for the foreseeable future. She and Henry were inexorably drifting apart, and she was relishing this new clandestine affair with Simon. It thrilled her to think they were completely on their own and no one knew about them. The interference of the outside world stopped whenever they met. It was just the two of them, and this secret hideaway just made everything all the more idyllic.

Simon found this affair with Charlene to be a pivotal point for him. The bisexual side of his nature was lately waning, as the sheer excitement and emotional fulfillment of being with Charlene was overpowering him. The guilt he felt was growing. But he determined to live with the hidden guilt rather than tell her the truth and suffer the shame of being exposed plus the guilt of wounding her.

So they sped off down the expressway, contented and perfected in each other's presence. They had risen to a new level of accord in the very short time they had known one another. They were still strongly attracted, but gone was the impatience because they already knew it was worth waiting for. Their hands touched. They were charged by the electricity as the hair on their arms rose and intertwined. Their sweet symbiosis of skin enraptured the two and the words from their lips made love in the air between them. The bouquet of their bodies carried them away to an island where all things are possible. He basked and she breathed, her beauty, and his brawn. In a moving vehicle their love had stilled the distance between them. As the landscape blurred behind them, their future focused ahead. They were more than a love story. They were the truth which created it.

Simon wondered how much longer his good friend, mentor and confessor would let him use his hideaway home. He knew he couldn't reveal to Charlene whose house it was. But he didn't know why. It didn't much matter, because they were together and that was the most important thing. That was the whole point of it all, of using Henry's home, to be together.

Charlene took directions well. Simon had made the drive last weekend and knew the way. She relied on Simon's geographical sense and memory because the GPS in her car was broken. It was disabled by Henry two months earlier. He promised to replace it. He promised a lot of things. She didn't care. The most important promise now was of a new life with her new man.

The Skater

When they parked the car in Henry's garage, Simon couldn't help but comment again about the strangeness of it. It was for all intents and purposes, a two and a half car garage, but it had only one single garage door into it. What he wasn't aware of was the contracting dispute between Henry and the builder who put the addition on his house. For three weeks Henry waited for the contractor to put in the doors. However, he kept stalling, saying he only had one door and was waiting on delivery of the other. Finally, Henry told him to install just the one door, wall up the other side, bring back the bricklayers and be done with it. He'd use it for storage space, he said. There were quite a few boxes in the garage that Simon hadn't noticed the week before.

Henry's final campsite on his journey home was near Jackson Mississippi. This time he would get a proper night's sleep, he told himself on Thursday when he arrived. He did.

He woke up well rested and very satisfied with the unexpected turn his life had taken. He would definitely do that again. He was addicted once more. This time, he wasn't only addicted to power, but to the power to hold life and death in his hands. Even the thought of flaring, dissimilar nostrils couldn't hold a candle to the ecstasy he experienced less than three days ago. Though secrecy was all important to him, his only unfulfilled wish was that he'd never be able to tell anyone how powerful he was. Not even his mother and she was the only one he would tell, if he could have.

He left Jackson for Baton Rouge about an hour before dusk. He had ample time to relax and eat on his trek home. He was in no hurry. Life was beautiful, and becoming more so with every recollection of his masterful performance in Toronto. He wondered if he could ever become a serial killer. Or, would his kills be limited to necessity and opportunity? He decided on the latter, but the former he held out as a possibility for research and study. Callous was his middle name.

"I can't believe the bye week's almost over," Murray said.

"At least it was a nice break, and now I've had a sneak peek at life in the slow lane."

"It's not a slow lane, Deb. It's an off-ramp."

"And where does that lead?"

"The intersection of dreams and wishes, where the on-ramp is closed for structural flaws."

After five days with Murray, golfing and fishing, Deborah was pooped. But it was a good pooped. They did more golfing than fishing, and that pleased her. The players were due to report back on Saturday, and all in all it looked like a playoff run was in the cards. She thought of cards, and those many years ago when Dino picked South Dakota. She thought of how she met Murray at the side of the road. Was it by chance? All the wonderful people and things in her life were due to a homemade game of relocation lottery. God had been very good to her and she gave thanks daily for her blessings, believing with all her heart that she was put there to receive them.

She would sell her team and move on. There would be more time for everything then. More time for Murray, the grandchildren, Dino, and most important, herself. What she didn't realize was that there wasn't more time and there never would be. She always did have all the time there was. Now, she would start using it better.

All day long Pamela envisaged the scenario that would take place at the airport. She wondered whether she should rush over to him when he came through customs. No, she thought, but she would certainly smile, move slowly in his direction and give him a warm, but platonic hug. Then, perhaps later in the evening they would touch hands, weaving their fingers together. Only then would they really, really know for sure, what they both already felt for sure, which was a breathtaking contentment in each other's presence.

What was the invisible reality that brought them together? She pondered that question all week long. She had spoken with him for less than five minutes yet she was smitten. Her consciousness had joyfully undergone a friendly takeover. The incorporation of her mind with his soul brought with it a familiar comfort, which strangely, she had never felt before. Was this a random harvest? Surely not, she thought. This was a yield of sweet corn, premeditated since before the seeds that brought it forth. There was no other good reason for the earth and the sky and the sun and the rain to be here. This was the only reason life existed at all. For without it, there was no point.

She had a silent knowing that he had already lived a life with her. Was that just wishful thinking? Or did that mental projection originate from before her, to cast its image on the landscape of her mind? She was sure this spot she had come to was a place of understanding, not ages but eons old. They had made the earth together and sewn the stars on the blanket of the galaxy. Was their karma about to expire at the birth of their return to each other?

She knew she would be with him soon. She already felt this strange nostalgia for the future, conceived in the womb of the past. She was a woman and thus trapped in the vessel of her kind, with doubts and fears and worries. But this wave of love and purity was cresting in the sea of passion. Of that, she had no doubt. The immutable truth that pushed them apart had matured into this intensity of love that would pull them back together.

The Skater

She smiled a lot that day, on duty. It wasn't one of her best days as a policewoman. Her mind wasn't much on policing. But it was her best day so far, as a woman.

Henry waited until twenty minutes past midnight before he drove down the dead end lane to his house. He parked in the driveway. The pickup was filled with building materials and other things he bought on his camping trip. He decided to unload the truck later. He didn't want to be heard making a racket in the garage.

He used the garage door opener to get inside the house. He raised the door only a couple of feet, just enough to crawl under. Then he lowered the door. He used Charlene's spare key to unlock her car. He jumped into the driver's seat. Turning the key to accessory started the radio and turned on the overhead light. The light he turned off but the radio he left on. He liked listening to a car radio late at night. It was the endless chatter he was interested in and where it came from. This wasn't quite the same thing, though, because usually he was out on the road driving in the dark when this somewhat sacred ritual was performed.

This night he was content to sit in the garage and listen for awhile. He could feel it all starting again, the exciting heart palpitations, the quivering nerve ends. This time it was even more intense than the last time, because he not only enjoyed it for what it was, but delighted in the anticipation of knowing what feelings were yet to come. He knew he needed to slow down the process he was initiating, so when the time came to adjudicate and eradicate he would be flawlessly calm. Savoring the sweetness of this act was all important to him.

The fervor and the ardor and the intensity of it all increased his level of tumescence far beyond anything he'd ever experienced before. Even a few days earlier when the Cameron problem was solved he hadn't reached this height of sexual arousal. A large stain was spreading across the 'big top' in his pants. He wondered aloud if he would be able to contain himself. He decided that he would. He would sit there, in her car, on her seat that had only hours earlier caressed her rainy gateway, and he would wait for the spontaneous propulsions to begin. The evidence would not be wiped away. The two fornicating sinners would see and stray no more before their god. Vengeance was his, said Henry.

He cast his mind back to yesterday, and how easy it was to score some high-quality heroin with a good connection like Wilbur Bjarno. He was a jack of all trades, was Wilbur. He was a part-time pimp and a full-time dealer who came to Henry for counseling as part of a plea bargain deal. He boasted to Henry about his climb up the ladder from his humble beginnings as a mule. Henry considered he may have once been a mule, but he was still a donkey. No matter, Wilbur, like all the other peasants, was very useful to him. Henry learned everything he needed to know about shooting up. Most important to Wilbur, and also to Henry, was the information about how not to overdose. Wilbur explained in great detail, how much was too much, even for a long time addict. Henry proved to be a precocious student as he prepared for his finals.

It was all becoming clear to him now, why he was so meticulous about gathering and storing information in his never-ending quest to out-anticipate the opponent. He felt as though he was in touch with a higher power, which encouraged him and led him to this present place, in a car, in a garage. But not in a hurry and not in a rage.

He called Simon from Charlene's cell phone. Six rings, and he didn't answer. He called again. He knew he never turned his cell phone off. He also knew Simon didn't know why he never turned it off.

"Hello."

"Simon, it's Henry. I need your help. Right away."

"Help with what?"

"Simon, I'm in the garage, my garage. I want you to come out to the garage."

"Now?"

"Now. Come out to the garage now. And don't wake your girlfriend."

"Okay."

Henry sat quietly waiting for Simon, listening to the radio. They were discussing Area 51, contrails and Bigfoot. He laughed out loud when he thought about a family of those large hairy beasts. Would it be proper to call them a Bigfoot family or a family of Bigfeet? He told himself to remember that one. That was a good one.

Simon opened the door into the garage. Henry turned the headlights on and off in the darkness, showing Simon he was in the car. Simon fumbled for a second or two, found the light switch and turned it on. He strode over to the vehicle. A giant of a man, he cast a large shadow as he moved under the naked incandescent light above him. Both front doors were ajar but Henry kicked the passenger door open a little further. The seat had already been lowered and moved all the way back because Simon had occupied it on their trip down from Shreveport. Henry had adjusted his seat also, but for more grave reasons.

As Simon bent over to open the door he noticed the rear passenger door was also ajar. Henry heard him say, "Shit, Charlene's always leaving her doors open." And with that he wiggled into the car like a cosmonaut into an old Soyuz space capsule. "Yeah, she has the same habit with her legs," Henry enunciated at the instant Simon's ass hit the leather seat. The lethal hypodermic needle entered Simon's carotid artery at 12:53 AM on

The Skater

Saturday. Eleven seconds later, Henry was the only one left in the car. Well, the only one alive.

Jon and Pamela were enjoying a happy and joyful weekend together. All the topics that new love begs to speak of were discussed. Religion, philosophy, politics and the like were wholeheartedly included, considering the very different backgrounds of these two. Age as well was on the agenda as Jon was nine years older than Pamela. Not that their age difference would have mattered. But the ramifications, in a cultural sense, was a point Jon wondered about aloud. Pamela assuaged his fears, telling him that in her culture it was quite acceptable for the man, she wanted to say husband, to be considerably older. For reasons of financial security and stability.

They talked long into the night about their beliefs. Not religious beliefs, but their spiritual understanding, stripped naked of religious and cultural dogma. It was a beautiful conversation for them both. They found more than just a little common ground. Huge tracts of rich and fertile lands lay fallow between them. They both believed that a loving force had brought them together. They quickly became singer songwriter to each other, each providing lyric and meaning to the other's voice.

They didn't spend the night together. So very much time and energy was expended in the embrace of their new spiritual union. An attempt, at that point, to draw their spirits down through the light spectrum and into the vibratory scale of physicality would have been too painful. This was a spiritual reunion of ancient souls, spinning a cocoon of pure love around themselves. This was the answer to every question ever uttered, in this or any other universe. This human veinous love trap would pass through the ends of eternity, and still survive, as it always had.

Then it was time for Pamela to leave, to go home and sleep, while Jon slept in his hotel room. They were to meet later in the day, she said. They would meet in their dreams as well, she said. In a bistro, overlooking canals and gondolas. Cappuccino and tiramisu on their table would wait awhile, as they looked and beheld in awe, the beauty of each other's soul.

They met again at 1 PM in the hotel lobby, just as she had suggested. They both knew for sure that whatever the future held for them, they would face it with humility and gratitude, together.

"Jeez, it's cold in here," Jon complained.

"Cold? Oh yeah, Florida, I forgot. You ain't seen nothing yet."

"Winter'll be ridiculous. You'll have to come south."

"You said you lived in Germany. Gets pretty cold there doesn't it?"

"Yeah, but I didn't go out much."

"Well, you'll just have to toughen up. There's plenty to do here. Open," Pamela said as she handed Jon a gift wrapped box.

"Gee, thanks, what is it?"

"Do you think I did all that wrapping so I could tell you what it is before you open it?"

" No, I guess not," Jon said as he tore away the paper and opened the box. "Wow, Pamela, thanks. But I can't even skate."

"You'll learn. I'll teach you. I think they'll fit. I guessed on the size. Your shoes looked about the same size as my brother's shoes."

"You shouldn't have, but thank you. These must have cost a fortune."

"Actually, although they look brand-new, they're really secondhand. I picked 'em up at the skate exchange yesterday."

They would have needed an electron microscope or a team of crime scene investigators to see the blood on them. Jon had originally gone to Toronto to spot and talk to Cam Timchuk. Now, little spots of Cam Timchuk were trying to talk to him.

Henry sat in the car for a full half hour before he finally began to think of Charlene. Prior to that he was in a state of bliss. The football players who consulted him talked of the 'zone'. He knew none of them would have been able to handle this place to which he had just come. Looking at the giant, hulking Simon beside him, he mouthed the sound "oooh." Once again feeling omniscient, he added the words omnipotent and omnipresent. His will was done.

No one in the land was finer than he, at that moment. On his whim alone, life was continued or concluded. Had he been able to feel like others, at that instant, he might well have felt something akin to sorrow for Simon. After all, he really liked the big guy, but he had to suffer the fate of those who crossed the King.

Leaving the garage, he stepped silently through the house. He anticipated Charlene, as she lay asleep in his bed. How fitting, he thought, that she would finally go where she had just come. It was very dark, no lights, no fluorescence, no LED, just a tiny hint of moonlight through the quarter closed blinds. Moving with rodent stealth, he approached her blanketed form until he could smell her skin. Her exhalations and heaving breasts excited him. He was rigid, and still swelling into his sperm soaked and rapidly caking underwear. What was happening to him? The timing of this was all wrong. He was beside himself with lust, but it hadn't happened this way with Simon or Cameron. He put the needle into his left hand as he turned to walk away from the bed and out of the room.

He headed back to the garage more aflame with each passing second. Why was he now, of all times, so feverishly lustful? Why did he want her now more than he had ever wanted her before? Was it because he was going to kill her? Or was it because he could smell her and hear her, but he could not see her? He gave long pause to the thought that everything might have changed for them, if he had only turned the light off.

The Skater

Opening the car door, he reached in to pull out Charlene's cell phone. He didn't know how long his excitement would last this time before the next sudden, electric discharge. He knew it would appear, like lightning out of the clear sky blue underwear. He was savoring it though, squeezing every second of rapture from his throbbing thoughts. He called Simon's cell phone and let it ring for minutes. Finally, in a fog, Charlene answered.

"Hello."
"Charlene."
"Henry?"
"Sorry to call so late. Where are you?"
"I'm.... at a friend's."
"Is Simon there?" Henry asked.
"Who? Who's Simon? What are you talking about?"
"Simon Leathem."
"Who is Simon Leathem?"
"You don't know him?" Henry loved turning the screw. It gave him great pleasure when people squirmed, especially when he was the cause of their discomfort.
"No. Never heard of him."
"Well, you're on his phone."
"What the hell's going on Henry?"
"Come to the garage. I'll explain."
"What?" Charlene started to shiver.
"Come and get your car," Henry ordered.
"Where are you? Where's Simon?"
"Oh, Simon? The guy you don't know. We're both in your car."

The phone was dropped on the bed and he heard her bare feet slapping on the hardwood. He sat and waited about twenty seconds until he heard the door open. Then he half climbed out of the car and looked at her. "Where's Simon?" she pleaded.

"Right here."

Henry stepped back, to allow her to get in the car from the driver's side. Her look of shock was what put him over the edge. For a few seconds, she might've been able to gain control of the situation. She could have locked herself in the car. His spare key was still in the ignition and the door opener was on the sun visor. She could have been screeching out just as he was screeching out. She could have been bolting like lightning out of there, while he was bolting like lightning in his underwear. But her new and true lover was dead in the passenger seat beside her and she was in panic and shock.

There were so many things he wanted to say to her. So many names he wanted to call her. This part wasn't working out either. Twice in the last three days he was God. Not this time, he didn't feel like God this time. This time it hurt him. He vowed never to let this happen again. If he couldn't punish her as a god, he would puncture her as a fallen angel. She passed with her arms wrapped around her future.

Henry left them both in the car, but only after he struggled to put Charlene into the backseat. It took him five minutes to get her all the way into the back so that he could shut the door. He needed a break. He was exhausted from the exertion, the executions, and his unexpected ejaculations. He removed his pants and underwear to examine the mess he was in. He threw them both into the back seat on top of Charlene. Her secrets and omissions would lie forever under his secretions and emissions. Clad only in his shirt, socks and shoes, he jumped into the front seat and fired up the engine. The door opener clicked. The garage door opened. He was going for a drive, a very short drive.

It had only taken him a few minutes to move the items from the closed side of the garage over to the open side, where the garage door was located. He stocked and stacked everything neatly against the wall, leaving plenty of room to maneuver the car. He had plenty of room to back Charlene's car about half way out of the garage. Then he moved the car forward turning into the empty left side, the side with no door. He pulled forward as far as he could. The vehicle was in a diagonal position, mostly in the closed side of the garage, but not entirely so. Inch by inch, and bit by bit he maneuvered the car backward and forward like a parallel parking nightmare. Finally, the entire car was in the closed side of the garage. There was a space of about two feet between the right side of the car and the middle of the garage. There was also a distance of about two feet between the left side of the car and the far wall.

He was exhausted from all his efforts. After all, he was not a strong man. He never actually thought of himself as a man anyway. He was just who he was. When he was a boy, he didn't think of himself as a boy. And now that he was a man he thought not of that either. What he did think of was the peculiar vacuous feeling in his groin from his rapid double evacuation. He lost a lot of fluid, and his penis felt sore at its glans and numb at its base.

He closed the garage door and walked over to the door leading into the house. Turning off the lights, he entered the house and headed for his liquor cabinet. Out from the cabinet came his most favored burgundy goblet followed and filled with ten ounces of his finest port. He smelled. He swirled. He swallowed. He poured himself another, feeling the effects of the first. He was dizzy from the port, and his head swam to his starboard side.

He went into the bedroom. He was going to take a shower but first he stood at the bedside where Charlene had just lain. He could still see the

The Skater

vague outline of her form on the 500 thread count sheets. The mattress had not yet fully recovered its shape. He kneeled down on the bed. Basking in her bouquet, he finished his port. Lying down, he clutched the sheets to his nose, smelling her for the last time alive, knowing the next time he smelled her it wouldn't be this sweet. He closed his eyes and slept for twenty minutes. He woke abruptly and showered speedily. As he scrubbed himself clean, he thought of nothing other than getting to an IHOP and taking some golf lessons soon.

Twelve noon on Monday saw Jon back at his desk, trying to catch up with events. All the Jaguar players were to have reported back by Saturday. They all did, except Simon Leathem. Jon discovered that Simon flew up to Shreveport on Friday. No one had seen him since. He knew about the work he was doing with his outreach program. So he made a number of calls to various people in an attempt to verify whether he actually arrived there on Friday. He hadn't. Jon was puzzled. Why would he fly to Shreveport on Friday if he had to report back with the team on Saturday? His flight didn't arrive in Shreveport until late Friday afternoon. It didn't make any sense to him. There must have been another reason he flew to Shreveport.

Coach Mann was furious. Deborah was at a loss to understand what was going on. As far she was concerned Simon was a rock. He was courteous, and he was a gentleman. She liked that. He was also a very spiritual man and she knew he would never, of his own volition, do a thing like this. He was the pivotal player on their offensive line. He was a leader both on and off the field. His backup was a rookie who had never played or even started a regular-season game. Everything would begin to unravel without Simon in the lineup. She knew that. Dave Mann knew that. Everyone knew that.

Henry knew that too. The hefty bet he placed against the Jaguars for next week's Monday night game was proof. Lots of money was still in the till, from his four unwitting contributors. Losing the big wager wouldn't bother him. And if he won, as he expected, it would just finance more investment. He really couldn't lose, and he was satisfied knowing that as he worked throughout the weekend.

And work, he did. After his refreshment break and short nap he got down to business in the garage. Joanna, who occupied the house all the previous week, took delivery of all the goods via UPS and FedEx that Henry ordered. These were some of the items that Henry had neatly piled against the wall. He half backed his pickup into the garage and began unloading it. Now it was time to start unpacking and setting up. He thought for a second or two about Alan Bean, the documentary he was watching when he killed himself, and the ancient Egyptians.

He read the instructions and began assembling hoses to tanks. He set the pressure valves as recommended. Opening the car door and pointing in the nozzle, he began spraying the two lifeless lovers with the most expensive, top end, concrete sealer available on the market. In his quick search of the web he learned there were two types of sealer. Breathable and non-breathable. He chose the latter, telling the order taker on the phone that the surface he would be spraying had a skin on it. The telephone operator assured him that no moisture would escape. Henry placed his order and made a mental note to locate the manufacturers.

He got immense satisfaction from spraying them. It reminded him of the time he sealed a deck as a summer work project. He felt artistic, like Van Gogh, but this wasn't a van and it wasn't going to go anywhere. When he was done, he was soaked with sweat. He found it difficult to breathe under the cumbersome mask. He took it off. They had such a lovely shine on them that they reminded him of a bug and a leaf encapsulated in tree sap.

While his two victims cured, he set about to do a little housecleaning. First on the agenda was gathering all the security tapes that had recorded Simon and Charlene. These would be thrown into the car, along with any of their personal belongings. Bed sheets, pillows, pillowcases, duvet, towels and face cloths, soap and shampoo and pretty much everything that wasn't nailed down in the bedroom area was put in the trunk of the car. The scrubbing and sanitizing he left for Joanna. She would be back on Monday morning.

He was meticulous. He really wasn't worried in the least about forensics testing, because that would only occur at a crime scene. Still, he dotted his i's and crossed his t's. No bodies, no car, no trace whatsoever would be left of them. No reason on earth existed for them to be at Henry's house anyway. A woman having an affair behind her fiancé's back wouldn't be doing it in his house, would she? She lived in Shreveport. Why would she drive four hours to Baton Rouge to screw somebody in the house of the person she was hiding it from? Henry was really pleased with how this was all playing out. Some of these explanations he was pondering for the very first time. Yet, it all had the appearance of a well rehearsed plot. In his mind, he gave himself credit for planning it all. In truth, it was just more shit luck.

Closed cell foam insulation was a remarkable product. It created an impermeable membrane wherever it was used. It didn't make any difference whether it was used around electrical sockets or eye sockets, the lip of a windowsill or the lip of a psychiatrist. It filled the gap. It was ironic, Henry thought, that all his life as a professional lineman, Simon had opened holes and now all of his were about to be closed.

The Skater

He leaned in and began spraying the insulation into the car from the open doors on the driver's side. He was relaxed and somewhat giddy from the sheer exhilaration of it all. This wasn't like offing some nobody hobo. These were two people who would be missed and soon the search would be on. Whether the two could be linked to each other didn't matter to him. They would be news talk fodder for a long time, Henry reckoned.

The insulation resembled angel food cake until it began hardening to look like that yellowish, hard candy with all the air bubbles in it. He couldn't remember what it was called, but he had a craving to eat some soon. He decided to look it up on the Internet, the felon friendly web, to find out what it was called. This was Henry's meditation process, if it could be called that. In less than a week, he had become addicted to killing. But the real thrill, he thought, would come later in avoiding detection and reveling in it.

He enjoyed the slow and deliberate process of encasing Simon and Charlene. Great care was taken to ensure all the vents and openings were plugged until the foam spilled out from inside the vehicle. The trunk was the final area of the car he insulated before beginning the last stage of his foam improvement project. Once finished with the interior of the car, he set up yet another tank and began spraying from the floor up. The entire space between the underside of the car and the floor was covered in the yellowcake, as was the entire car itself. The sealer and insulation covered the bulk of their bodies. But any part of their carcasses which touched the upholstery would soon rot. That was why he filled the cavity between the car and the floor. And just to round things out, he encased the whole vehicle. By the time he was finished, he couldn't see the car at all. A massive wad of yellow chewing gum was what it looked like to Henry, as he doubled his pleasure and doubled his fun.

CHAPTER 15

By mid-week the Jaguar's starting center was front-page news. Much speculation abounded throughout the league. Foul play was beginning to emerge as a distinct possibility among football aficionados. There were reports that Simon had been seen at various locations throughout the country. The fake sightings just added to the hype and the hype fueled the frustrations of the Jaguar players and management. Things were coming unglued in Jacksonville.

Charlene Kempf-Klassen was a different story. It wasn't until Wednesday that the police became involved. Her office called her parents and her parents called Henry. Nobody seemed to know where she could have gone. Henry reminded her father that Charlene was quite attached to her car and was most likely still in it, somewhere. Where she was, he couldn't hazard a guess but he told him she spent so much time at work that she was likely just resting someplace. Throughout her life she always preferred the role of heroine, he told him. This would be no different, he said. Eventually, he told him, everyone would see the same heroin in her that he saw. Henry enjoyed his disingenuous consolation and didn't forget to surreptitiously remind her father that she had never been to Henry's house.

The two cops who showed up at his office the following week were typically cynical. Henry knew from the get-go that these two detectives were very suspicious of him. He concluded it was because of his diminutive size, his carriage and his demeanor. After all, there wasn't a shred of evidence that he was involved in her disappearance. Another couple of big guys to play like fiddles, he thought.

Byron Harrison and Jake Prudhomme looked less like fiddles and more like cellos, big and loud with deep resonant voices. They were both nearing retirement and they both relished the thought of it. They had even talked of getting into some joint venture together, once they retired from the force but nothing concrete was ever planned. Most likely, they'd see each other less and less until it would become much easier to isolate than integrate and much harder to have fun than to just remember it.

The two detectives silently made their assessments of Henry Collier. Both men felt he was a chronic whiner, a supercilious snob and a narcissist to be sure. Their conclusion? A skinny little prick, the likes of which they'd seen many times before.

Actually, they'd never seen anyone quite like Henry before, and their belief that they had was testament to his clever malevolence. Good cops, bad cops were just clusters of clowns to him. Pissed up cop, pissed off cop, happy clown, sad clown, but clowns nonetheless. He would have them jumping into the barrel soon enough.

"Have you found out anything about Charlene yet?"

"No. Is there anything you can tell us that might shed some light on her whereabouts?" Byron responded.

"No. I haven't seen her for weeks. We've both been pretty busy."

"Were you having problems?" Jake asked Henry.

"No, we just haven't seen each other for a while. And why would you say, 'were you having problems'? Are you implying you think she's dead?"

"No I'm not implying that at all. I'm asking if you were having problems prior to her disappearance," Jake said as he caught a glimpse of Byron. He realized he had just made a mistake and this little wimp nailed him for it.

"Thank God," Henry feigned praying, acting very distressed.

Byron, realizing how sharp this person of interest and possible suspect was, took over the questioning, which gave Jake an opportunity to regroup. It was clear to both Byron and Jake that their interviewee would be obdurate and difficult whenever he had the opportunity. They endeavored to afford him as few opportunities as possible.

Out in the car, Jake looked at Byron and asked him what he thought of Henry. "An arrogant little cock sucker," filled the enclosed space between them. "Yeah, that's what I think too."

"D'you think he's involved?"

"Who knows? That reporter sure thinks so."

Jon Buchanan was the only person who even considered there might be a link between Charlene Kempf-Klassen and Simon Leathem. So far, no one else agreed with him. He was on his own on this one. Even Byron Harrison and Jake Prudhomme couldn't get too excited about Jon's suspicions. Jon wanted immediate access to the airport security cameras, but was held up by his editor. He told him to wait a few days to see if any other leads developed. They didn't. And the security cameras showed nothing conclusive. Only that Simon arrived in Shreveport and made his way to an unidentified vehicle.

The Skater

As driven, dedicated and energetic as Jon was, he was still in a newly minted dreamland of his own making. He was head over heels, and ass over tea kettle in love with Pamela. He had never felt like this before and his new young love had him distracted, but happy. In fact, he'd never in his life been so pleased or resigned about not getting to the bottom of something. Love had certainly softened his outlook on life. Since Jon believed nothing happened accidentally, and events unfolded according to some unknown ethereal plan, he would have been befuddled by his own temporary lack of tenacity. The very lack he exhibited might well make Henry Collier his unknowing beneficiary.

The visit by the police didn't upset Henry. He was waiting for their visit and their interview, and their attendant suspicions. Perhaps because of their visit, though, he considered leaving the office early just to celebrate. He changed his mind when he realized that an early departure from work would look suspicious, should anyone have been monitoring his comings and goings.

In his world, every single action was calculated to appear a certain way, no matter what his intentions were. He lived his life as if someone was always watching him. It was a paranoia born of his peculiar psychopathy. He was created by his environment. He was a coward, and therefore would go to great lengths to avoid detection. He thought he had it all. He thought he was free. He wasn't. He was actually enslaved by his own counterfeit emancipation. He knew of no other way to live. To forfeit his illusion of freedom represented death, and he was fearful in the extreme.

So, he didn't leave work early. He left at the usual time. He was beginning to feel like an actor in a movie. Not just any movie and not just any actor. No, he was a giant actor much, much larger than life appearing in an epic, the greatest story ever told. The Henry Collier story.

The next scene in his epic showed him pulling into his garage. The door closed behind his vehicle. As he stepped out of the truck he was confronted by his own flawless handiwork. No BMW. No large yellow piece of hard candy. And no brilliant red bow on the top. Just a seamless, flawless white garage wall. Perfect, he was almost thankful for summer jobs. Drywalling seemed to suit Henry's innate ability to work with his hands. He was good at it and probably could have made a good living in the construction business. But he knew even way back then that he was born to tinker. And nothing required more tinkering than the sordid cesspools inside people's heads. Not his, of course. His was a clear, sparkling spring of limitless possibilities for advantage and countless opportunities for their execution. It fit him, that word, he mused. He decided to use the word as much as possible for the next little while, the word execution. It would serve as his cowardly signature, and he knew it wouldn't be lost on the police. They would know when they were being told to fuck off. But, like Alan Bean, they could do nothing at all about it.

Deborah Dececchi had a crisis on her hands. Her Pro-Bowl center was AWOL, and the entire country, it seemed, was focused on his sudden and unexplained disappearance. It had also come to her attention that several players had invested in some kind of speculative business deal with Henry. She sensed her team on the verge of a meltdown. Coaching staff and players were being questioned by the police. Henry was being questioned in both the disappearance of her star lineman, and his own fiancée.

After much soul-searching, and a lot of consternation, she decided to call in Henry. He was clearly in contravention of his contract, which specifically banned any business dealings with the players he consulted. And being questioned in two separate disappearances didn't increase his stock with her either. The only sensible course of action, she felt, was to terminate his contract forthwith and make short shrift of him. Performance specialist, be damned. She now saw the evidence so many in her organization complained about earlier. This shrink was a cancer on her team.

Henry was a cancer. He was also a murderer. He should have been in a cell in isolation. Instead, the mutant cells of his psyche continued to metastasize as he plotted even more. Waiting to be summoned into Deborah's office, he played through a couple of scenarios in his head. What would he do if she fired him? He knew that was a real possibility. If she did fire him, at least he'd be able to continue his relationship with the players he was embezzling. Or would he? She had a great deal of leverage over them and they wouldn't jeopardize their own contracts. He was sure of that.

He could see it all slipping away now. The money, the Cayman's, the babes, the sexy snorting lifestyle he held in such esteem. The lifestyle to which he was now so very accustomed. He quickly retooled and started producing the new thoughts that would be his vehicle to a better life. After all, it wasn't as fulfilling as he thought it would be, he told himself. Sure, he enjoyed the constant tension with the police, but it didn't seem to be a fair fight. Not that there was anything fair about Henry. He was way ahead of them and they would never catch up. Of that, he was certain. In order to really enjoy the game he needed more risk. But risk required courage and that he didn't have.

So, he resigned himself to be conciliatory and accept whatever fate came his way. Good thing for him too, because he was out the door without it hitting him in the ass real quick indeed. That was okay. They were still obligated to pay out his contract. He took solace in that. Money for nothing, he was ecstatic.

While Mr. and Mrs. Gerry Kempf enlisted the help of a renowned psychic in their desperate attempt for an answer to their daughter's fate,

The Skater

the police were concerned with Henry's recent purchase of suspicious building materials. They thought they were on to something, too. Until they were confronted with every single item Henry had purchased. It was all there, the tanks, the drywall, everything. All unused. All unopened. Much of it still shrink-wrapped. Most important were the receipts Henry smugly provided. Receipts accounting for every single purchase. Exact, corresponding receipts, they were all there. Their case was falling apart, with weeks having passed and no new leads. As far as the police were concerned, Henry was still a person of interest and a possible suspect. But unless something new came up the disappearance of Charlene Kempf-Klassen would remain unsolved.

Many years prior, Johnny Collier, unwittingly, taught his son a very valuable lesson. Watching his father's sleight of hand prepared him well for all his future clandestine endeavors. Alcoholics were good for something, even if they were only good for object lessons in compulsive pathological behavior. And Henry was an astute student of the human condition.

The constant tension in the Collier household always revolved around Johnny's drinking. Edith knew how much he drank and knew how much it cost her family, both financially and emotionally. Though she tiptoed around her husband, and pretended not to notice, she always kept an eye on the rate at which the bottles were being emptied. Henry, privy to this cat and mouse game, saw many times how his father outwitted his mother simply by making double, and sometimes triple, purchases of his treasured alcohol. With the unknown bottles hidden, Johnny had two avenues to drink with impunity. He could either drink from both bottles at the same time or he could switch bottles at opportune moments. Either way, his wife was none the wiser about his double consumption of booze.

So it was with Henry, that very same principle employed to create the illusion that the purchase of materials was made, but nothing was used. He always believed that a cashless society would infringe on his personal freedom. Following the money, the infamous paper trail, was the accepted way to get at the truth. Henry knew that the only paper with no trail was paper money. With cash, he bought everything he needed to use and with credit, he bought everything needed for his ruse. "Thanks, dad," was all he could say.

"I hear a noise, a ringing noise, a phone. It's ringing," Phyllis Graham said. "But where am I? In bed, but not my bed, not my house. But it's familiar. I've been here before."

Phyllis Graham, employing a photograph of Charlene Kempf-Klassen, along with two personal items, seemed to be reliving Charlene's last earthly moments. "I'm in a garage. My car. I see my car and my fiancé. He's dead. My boyfriend's dead. I feel a stabbing in my neck. He's killing me. Killed us both. I feel two people. Three energies. Very confusing. I'm getting no sense of location, I'm sorry. I'm in a house, I've been in it before. With him. Not his house, though."

Jake Prudhomme hit the stop button and looked at Byron. "What in the name of God do you make of that?"

"Very confusing is right."

"No shit."

"Let's see," Byron calculated. "Two people, three 'energies'. What does that mean? The third one is the killer? One's a dual personality, maybe? Or, one person's dead and two are still alive? Does a dead body emanate energy?"

"I wouldn't think so. Maybe."

"She said her fiancé's dead."

Jake and Byron held a stare for a few seconds. It was a familiar stare. It was the stare of experience, instinct and intuition. They both knew Henry smelled. "Yeah, and if we ever were to give any weight to this psychic reading, we'd have to eliminate Collier as a suspect."

"Yeah, we would."

They never did contact Phyllis Graham, believing they would only receive more confusing or ambiguous information. What a strange twist of fate in Henry's favor that was. In not wanting to eliminate Henry as a possible suspect, they had just eliminated any hope of ever catching him. Their one tiny error in language perception would eventually let him off the hook. They thought the words 'he's dead' referred to Henry, the fiancé, thinking that the fiancé and boyfriend were the same person. And so they were unwilling to investigate further, precisely because of their gut instincts that he was somehow involved. Their egos delivered a fatal blow to their intuition, and Henry was the lucky winner of the stay out of jail lottery.

It wasn't too long before the police investigation was relegated to the cold case files. The disappearance of Charlene Kempf-Klassen remained a mystery, and the investigation into the disappearance of Simon Leathem concluded with the same fate. There was no evidence to link the two disappearances to each other. Except that they had known each other and had both last been seen in Shreveport. Other than that, nothing.

The Jaguars imploded through the last half of the season and finished at the bottom of their division. The offensive line lacked cohesion, fell apart, and Simon was missed in the locker room. The funny thing that coaches and commentators and analysts alike couldn't come to grips with was why all the skill position players performed so poorly. No one dared to believe that the sub par performance of those players was in any way linked to the absence of their performance specialist. No one, except Henry.

If players had come to believe he could make them play better, which they did, they would also believe, unbeknownst to them, that he could make them play worse. He knew very well that anyone who accepts praise from another as truth will undoubtedly be buoyed by positive emotions. He also knew that the very process of believing praise to be the truth has its shadow side. A subliminal scolding would be accepted as truth. A casual doubt, cast in one's direction, would by virtue of this psychic process, be believed to be the truth.

Feeling the heat from the police weeks earlier and hearing the scuttlebutt about impending organizational changes, Henry began his war of psychological sabotage. He had his own gut feeling that he wouldn't be around the football team much longer. No more dreams of inebriated fornication fests. He aimed to screw up the players and the team with a little tinkering shrinkage. The pathetic performances of all the players involved during the last few weeks of the season only served to enhance his reputation as a performance guru. When he was released by the team they took a nosedive. So, it became a popular myth amongst football players and fans alike that Henry's absence accounted for the team's poor play.

He went back to his practice in Baton Rouge and assumed his role as psychologist to the normal folk. He needed a rest anyway. He'd done a lot of traveling since his foray into the football world began. He'd also done a yeoman's job of murdering people. And, though it tired him, it also excited and motivated him. He palpitated and salivated over his mental imagery of murders past, and murders yet to come. What would his next murderous orgasm be like? He could hardly wait.

Jon Buchanan was back in Toronto for awhile, still in love with Pamela. They planned to marry as soon as her family accepted him. It was a slow and torturous process, but they knew it had to be done. Neither one of them was in a hurry. As long as they held each other's love they could wait as long as it took.

Jon never did get very far with his personal investigation into the Simon Leathem disappearance. But he remained convinced that it was tied to Charlene's. He also still believed Henry to be right in the middle of it all.

"Hey, you're definitely getting better," Pamela shouted as Jon struggled to maintain his balance and steady himself on the ice. "You're somewhere else, what is it?"

"Henry Collier."

"Still? Can't you let that go? It's all over. Case closed."

"I'll keep diggin.'"

"What for?"

"I don't know. Just need to," Jon was perplexed, himself.

"And you think you can prove something? Uncover something?"

"Yeah, maybe. He's not gonna skate on me," Jon said, as he precariously tried to balance himself atop the murder weapons. Pretty soon, there'd be no DNA left on them. That hardly mattered because it was extremely unlikely anyone would ever consider the possibility.

It was the first Sunday in February and Henry sat down to watch the big game just before six o'clock. His drink of choice this day was rum and ginger beer. He planned to drink the entire forty ounces by the end of the third quarter. He also knew he would need to switch mixes somewhere along the line. He didn't have enough ginger beer. Just after seven o'clock the phone rang. He didn't answer it. That's what machines were for, anyway. Besides, he was having a blast, drinking and spectating.

Monday morning came. His head felt like a football. After he'd finished the rum, he got stuck into some wine too. Hangovers usually eluded him but this particular 'morning after' was a bad one. Until he played back the message from the night before.

"Henry? How do you do? My name is Meena Khan. I'm a close friend of your mother. Now, she doesn't know I'm calling. I don't want to worry her. So this is just between you and me, okay? A few months back, before we took our trip to Aruba? Well, I had a security camera installed in your mother's garage. Concealed. There is a particular tape you might be interested in. I still have it. It's in a safe place, not here of course. Maybe you'll want to give me a call so we can make some kind of arrangement? Oh, and before I forget, I'm always forgetting things, I forgot to put the garbage out when we got back. My number should be on your call display. You know your mother's number anyway."

Slowly but surely, over the next two hours Henry's headache lifted. His spirits soared. He thanked his higher power for this new opportunity he had been given. He felt alive and optimistic about his future. He only had one unanswered question left on his mind. "When does the ice melt on Lake Ontario?"

THE END